D0188418

DOVER · THRIFT · EDITIONS

Great Ghost Stories

EDITED BY JOHN GRAFTON

DOVER PUBLICATIONS, INC.
New York

DOVER THRIFT EDITIONS

GENERAL EDITOR: STANLEY APPELBAUM
EDITOR OF THIS VOLUME: PHILIP SMITH

Selection and editorial matter copyright © 1992 by Dover Publications, Inc.
All rights reserved under Pan American and International Copyright Conventions.

Published in Canada by General Publishing Company, Ltd., 30 Lesmill Road, Don Mills, Toronto, Ontario.
Published in the United Kingdom by Constable and Company, Ltd., 3 The Lanchesters, 162–164 Fulham Palace Road, London W6 9ER.

Great Ghost Stories is an original anthology of previously published material, first published by Dover Publications, Inc., in 1992. "The Monkey's Paw" is reprinted by permission of The Society of Authors as the literary representative of the Estate of W. W. Jacobs.

Manufactured in the United States of America
Dover Publications, Inc., 31 East 2nd Street, Mineola, N.Y. 11501

Library of Congress Cataloging-in-Publication Data

Great ghost stories / edited by John Grafton.
        p.   cm. — (Dover thrift editions)
    Includes bibliographical references.
    ISBN 0-486-27270-2
    1. Ghost stories, English.   2. Ghost stories, American.   I. Grafton, John.   II. Series.
PR1309.G5G73   1992
823'.0873308—dc20
                                                                92–20640
                                                                     CIP

Note

THE TEN GHOST STORIES reprinted here were first published in England and America between 1864 and 1912, a half-century that represents the golden age of this endlessly entertaining branch of popular fiction. So popular were ghost stories in the late Victorian and Edwardian periods that a selection such as this can only represent a sampling of the subcategories of the genre—from the subtle and the humorous to the chilling and the macabre, from the fictional historical account to the tale set in the contemporary world of everyday life. All of these will be found here by a range of authors from Charles Dickens, for whom an occasional ghost story was an interlude in his main literary work, to J. S. LeFanu and M. R. James, surely the greatest, respectively, nineteenth- and twentieth-century practitioners of the form. In a collection that could have been expanded many times with no diminution in quality, the only principle of selection was that the stories should be entertaining in themselves, and representative of the best the genre has to offer.

"The Phantom Coach" by Amelia B. Edwards (1831–1892) was first published in *All the Year Round*, a periodical edited by Charles Dickens, Christmas Number, 1864.

"To Be Taken with a Grain of Salt" by Charles Dickens (1812–1870) was first published in *All the Year Round*, Christmas Number, 1865.

"Dickon the Devil" by J. S. LeFanu (1814–1873) was first published in *London Society*, 1872.

"The Judge's House" by Bram Stoker (1847–1912) was first published in *Illustrated Sporting and Dramatic Life*, December 1891.

"A Ghost Story" by Jerome K. Jerome (1859–1927) was first published in *The Idler*, September 1892 as part of the serial *Novel Notes*. The title is the present editor's.

"The Moonlit Road" by Ambrose Bierce (1842–ca.1914) was first published in 1894.

"The Monkey's Paw" by W. W. Jacobs (1863–1943) was first published in *Harper's Monthly Magazine,* September 1902.

"The Rose Garden" by M. R. James (1862–1936) was first published in *More Ghost Stories of an Antiquary,* 1911.

"Bone to His Bone" by E. G. Swain (1861–1938) was first published in *The Stoneground Ghost Tales, Compiled from the Recollections of the Reverend Roland Batchel, Vicar of the Parish,* 1912.

"The Confession of Charles Linkworth" by E. F. Benson (1867–1940) was first published in *The Room in the Tower and Other Stories,* 1912.

Contents

The Phantom Coach

AMELIA B. EDWARDS

THE CIRCUMSTANCES I am about to relate to you have truth to recommend them. They happened to myself, and my recollection of them is as vivid as if they had taken place only yesterday. Twenty years, however, have gone by since that night. During those twenty years I have told the story to but one other person. I tell it now with a reluctance which I find it difficult to overcome. All I entreat, meanwhile, is that you will abstain from forcing your own conclusions upon me. I want nothing explained away. I desire no arguments. My mind on this subject is quite made up, and, having the testimony of my own senses to rely upon, I prefer to abide by it.

Well! It was just twenty years ago, and within a day or two of the end of the grouse season. I had been out all day with my gun, and had had no sport to speak of. The wind was due east; the month, December; the place, a bleak wide moor in the far north of England. And I had lost my way. It was not a pleasant place in which to lose one's way, with the first feathery flakes of a coming snowstorm just fluttering down upon the heather, and the leaden evening closing in all around. I shaded my eyes with my hand, and stared anxiously into the gathering darkness, where the purple moorland melted into a range of low hills, some ten or twelve miles distant. Not the faintest smoke-wreath, not the tiniest cultivated patch, or fence, or sheep-track, met my eyes in any direction. There was nothing for it but to walk on, and take my chance of finding what shelter I could, by the way. So I shouldered my gun again, and pushed wearily forward; for I had been on foot since an hour after daybreak, and had eaten nothing since breakfast.

Meanwhile, the snow began to come down with ominous steadiness, and the wind fell. After this, the cold became more intense, and the night came rapidly up. As for me, my prospects darkened with the darkening sky, and my heart grew heavy as I thought how my young wife was already watching for me through the window of our little inn parlour, and thought of all the suffering in store for her throughout this weary night. We had been married four months, and, having spent our autumn in the Highlands, were now lodging in a remote little village situated just on the verge of the great English moorlands. We were very much in love, and, of course, very happy. This morning, when we parted, she had implored me to return before dusk, and I had promised her that I would. What would I not have given to have kept my word!

1

Even now, weary as I was, I felt that with a supper, an hour's rest, and a guide, I might still get back to her before midnight, if only guide and shelter could be found.

And all this time, the snow fell and the night thickened. I stopped and shouted every now and then, but my shouts seemed only to make the silence deeper. Then a vague sense of uneasiness came upon me, and I began to remember stories of travellers who had walked on and on in the falling snow until, wearied out, they were fain to lie down and sleep their lives away. Would it be possible, I asked myself, to keep on thus through all the long dark night? Would there not come a time when my limbs must fail, and my resolution give way? When I, too, must sleep the sleep of death. Death! I shuddered. How hard to die just now, when life lay all so bright before me! How hard for my darling, whose whole loving heart——but that thought was not to be borne! To banish it, I shouted again, louder and longer, and then listened eagerly. Was my shout answered, or did I only fancy that I heard a far-off cry? I hallooed again, and again the echo followed. Then a wavering speck of light came suddenly out of the dark, shifting, disappearing, growing momentarily nearer and brighter. Running towards it at full speed, I found myself, to my great joy, face to face with an old man and a lantern.

'Thank God!' was the exclamation that burst involuntarily from my lips.

Blinking and frowning, he lifted his lantern and peered into my face. 'What for?' growled he, sulkily.

'Well—for you. I began to fear I should be lost in the snow.'

'Eh, then, folks do get cast away hereabout fra' time to time, an' what's to hinder you from bein' cast away likewise, if the Lord's so minded?'

'If the Lord is so minded that you and I shall be lost together, friend, we must submit,' I replied; 'but I don't mean to be lost without you. How far am I now from Dwolding?'

'A gude twenty mile, more or less.'

'And the nearest village?'

'The nearest village is Wyke, an' that's twelve mile t'other side.'

'Where do you live, then?'

'Out yonder,' said he, with a vague jerk of the lantern.

'You're going home, I presume?'

'Maybe I am.'

'Then I'm going with you.'

The old man shook his head, and rubbed his nose reflectively with the handle of the lantern.

'It ain't o' no use,' growled he. 'He 'ont let you in—not he.'

'We'll see about that,' I replied, briskly. 'Who is He?'

'The master.'

'Who is the master?'

'That's nowt to you,' was the unceremonious reply.

'Well, well; you lead the way, and I'll engage that the master shall give me shelter and a supper tonight.'

'Eh, you can try him!' muttered my reluctant guide; and, still shaking his head, he hobbled, gnome-like, away through the falling snow. A large mass loomed up presently out of the darkness, and a huge dog rushed out, barking furiously.

'Is this the house?' I asked.

'Ay, it's the house. Down, Bey!' And he fumbled in his pocket for the key.

I drew up close behind him, prepared to lose no chance of entrance, and saw in the little circle of light shed by the lantern that the door was heavily studded with iron nails, like the door of a prison. In another minute he had turned the key and I had pushed past him into the house.

Once inside, I looked round with curiosity, and found myself in a great raftered hall, which served, apparently, a variety of uses. One end was piled to the roof with corn, like a barn. The other was stored with flour-sacks, agricultural implements, casks, and all kinds of miscellaneous lumber; while from the beams overhead hung rows of hams, flitches, and bunches of dried herbs for winter use. In the centre of the floor stood some huge object gauntly dressed in a dingy wrapping-cloth, and reaching half way to the rafters. Lifting a corner of this cloth, I saw, to my surprise, a telescope of very considerable size, mounted on a rude movable platform, with four small wheels. The tube was made of painted wood, bound round with bands of metal rudely fashioned; the speculum, so far as I could estimate its size in the dim light, measured at least fifteen inches in diameter. While I was yet examining the instrument, and asking myself whether it was not the work of some self-taught optician, a bell rang sharply.

'That's for you,' said my guide, with a malicious grin. 'Yonder's his room.'

He pointed to a low black door at the opposite side of the hall. I crossed over, rapped somewhat loudly, and went in, without waiting for an invitation. A huge, white-haired old man rose from a table covered with books and papers, and confronted me sternly.

'Who are you?' said he. 'How came you here? What do you want?'

'James Murray, barrister-at-law. On foot across the moor. Meat, drink, and sleep.'

He bent his bushy brows into a portentous frown.

'Mine is not a house of entertainment,' he said, haughtily. 'Jacob, how dared you admit this stranger?'

'I didn't admit him,' grumbled the old man. 'He followed me over the muir, and shouldered his way in before me. I'm no match for six foot two.'

'And pray, sir, by what right have you forced an entrance into my house?'

'The same by which I should have clung to your boat, if I were drowning. The right of self-preservation.'

'Self-preservation?'

'There's an inch of snow on the ground already,' I replied, briefly; 'and it would be deep enough to cover my body before daybreak.'

He strode to the window, pulled aside a heavy black curtain, and looked out.

'It is true,' he said. 'You can stay, if you choose, till morning. Jacob, serve the supper.'

With this he waved me to a seat, resumed his own, and became at once absorbed in the studies from which I had disturbed him.

I placed my gun in a corner, drew a chair to the hearth, and examined my quarters at leisure. Smaller and less incongruous in its arrangements than the hall, this room contained, nevertheless, much to awaken my curiosity. The floor was carpetless. The whitewashed walls were in parts scrawled over with strange diagrams, and in others covered with shelves crowded with philosophical instruments, the uses of many of which were unknown to me. On one side of the fireplace, stood a bookcase filled with dingy folios; on the other, a small organ, fantastically decorated with painted carvings of medieval saints and devils. Through the half-opened door of a cupboard at the further end of the room, I saw a long array of geological specimens, surgical preparations, crucibles, retorts, and jars of chemicals; while on the mantelshelf beside me, amid a number of small objects, stood a model of the solar system, a small galvanic battery, and a microscope. Every chair had its burden. Every corner was heaped high with books. The very floor was littered over with maps, casts, papers, tracings, and learned lumber of all conceivable kinds.

I stared about me with an amazement increased by every fresh object upon which my eyes chanced to rest. So strange a room I had never seen; yet seemed it stranger still, to find such a room in a lone farmhouse amid those wild and solitary moors! Over and over again, I looked from my host to his surroundings, and from his surroundings back to my host, asking myself who and what he could be? His head was singularly fine; but it was more the head of a poet than of a philosopher. Broad in the temples, prominent over the eyes, and clothed with a rough profusion of perfectly white hair, it had all the ideality and much of the ruggedness that characterises the head of Louis von Beethoven. There were the same deep lines about the mouth, and the same stern furrows in the brow. There was the same concentration of expression. While I was yet observing him, the door opened, and Jacob brought in the supper. His master then closed his book, rose, and with more courtesy of manner than he had yet shown, invited me to the table.

A dish of ham and eggs, a loaf of brown bread, and a bottle of admirable sherry, were placed before me.

'I have but the homeliest farmhouse fare to offer you, sir,' said my entertainer. 'Your appetite, I trust, will make up for the deficiencies of our larder.'

I had already fallen upon the viands, and now protested, with the enthusiasm of a starving sportsman, that I had never eaten anything so delicious.

He bowed stiffly, and sat down to his own supper, which consisted, primitively, of a jug of milk and a basin of porridge. We ate in silence, and, when we had done, Jacob removed the tray. I then drew my chair back to the fireside. My host, somewhat to my surprise, did the same, and turning abruptly towards me, said:

'Sir, I have lived here in strict retirement for three-and-twenty years. During that time, I have not seen as many strange faces, and I have not read a single newspaper. You are the first stranger who has crossed my threshold for more than four years. Will you favour me with a few words of information respecting that outer world from which I have parted company so long?'

'Pray interrogate me,' I replied. 'I am heartily at your service.'

He bent his head in acknowledgment, leaned forward, with his elbows resting on his knees and his chin supported in the palms of his hands; stared fixedly into the fire; and proceeded to question me.

His inquiries related chiefly to scientific matters, with the later progress of which, as applied to the practical purposes of life, he was almost wholly unacquainted. No student of science myself, I replied as well as my slight information permitted; but the task was far from easy, and I was much relieved when, passing from interrogation to discussion, he began pouring forth his own conclusions upon the facts which I had been attempting to place before him. He talked, and I listened spellbound. He talked till I believe he almost forgot my presence, and only thought aloud. I had never heard anything like it then; I have never heard anything like it since. Familiar with all systems of all philosophies, subtle in analysis, bold in generalisation, he poured forth his thoughts in an uninterrupted stream, and, still leaning forward in the same moody attitude with his eyes fixed upon the fire, wandered from topic to topic, from speculation to speculation, like an inspired dreamer. From practical science to mental philosophy; from electricity in the wire to electricity in the nerve; from Watts to Mesmer, from Mesmer to Reichenbach, from Reichenbach to Swedenborg, Spinoza, Condillac, Descartes, Berkeley, Aristotle, Plato, and the Magi and mystics of the East, were transitions which, however bewildering in their variety and scope, seemed easy and harmonious upon his lips as sequences in music. By-and-by—I forget now by what link of conjecture or illustration—he passed on to that field which lies beyond the boundary line of even conjectural philosophy, and reaches no man knows whither. He spoke of the soul and its aspirations; of the spirit and its powers; of second sight; of prophecy; of those phenomena which, under the names of ghosts, spectres, and supernatural appearances, have been denied by the sceptics and attested by the credulous, of all ages.

'The world,' he said, 'grows hourly more and more sceptical of all that lies beyond its own narrow radius; and our men of science foster the fatal tendency. They condemn as fable all that resists experiment. They reject as false all that cannot be brought to the test of the laboratory or the dissecting-room. Against what superstition have they waged so long and obstinate a war, as against the belief in apparitions? And yet what superstition has maintained its hold upon the minds of men so long and so firmly? Show me any fact in physics, in history, in archæology, which is supported by testimony so wide and so various. Attested by all races of men, in all ages, and in all climates, by the soberest sages of antiquity, by the rudest savage of today, by the Christian, the Pagan, the Pantheist, the Materialist, this phenomenon is treated as a nursery tale by the philosophers of our century. Circumstantial evidence weighs with them as a feather in the balance. The comparison of causes with effects, however valuable in physical science, is put aside as worthless and unreliable. The evidence of competent witnesses, however conclusive in a court of justice, counts for nothing. He who pauses before he pronounces, is condemned as a trifler. He who believes, is a dreamer or a fool.'

He spoke with bitterness, and, having said thus, relapsed for some minutes into silence. Presently he raised his head from his hands, and added, with an altered voice and manner,

'I, sir, paused, investigated, believed, and was not ashamed to state my convictions to the world. I, too, was branded as a visionary, held up to ridicule by my contemporaries, and hooted from that field of science in which I had laboured with honour during all the best years of my life. These things happened just three-and-twenty years ago. Since then, I have lived as you see me living now, and the world has forgotten me, as I have forgotten the world. You have my history.'

'It is a very sad one,' I murmured, scarcely knowing what to answer.

'It is a very common one,' he replied. 'I have only suffered for the truth, as many a better and wiser man has suffered before me.'

He rose, as if desirous of ending the conversation, and went over to the window.

'It has ceased snowing,' he observed, as he dropped the curtain, and came back to the fireside.

'Ceased!' I exclaimed, starting eagerly to my feet. 'Oh, if it were only possible—but no! it is hopeless. Even if I could find my way across the moor, I could not walk twenty miles tonight.'

'Walk twenty miles tonight!' repeated my host. 'What are you thinking of?'

'Of my wife,' I replied, impatiently. 'Of my young wife, who does not know that I have lost my way, and who is at this moment breaking her heart with suspense and terror.'

'Where is she?'

'At Dwolding, twenty miles away.'

'At Dwolding,' he echoed, thoughtfully. 'Yes, the distance, it is true, is twenty miles; but—are you so very anxious to save the next six or eight hours?'

'So very, very anxious, that I would give ten guineas at this moment for a guide and a horse.'

'Your wish can be gratified at a less costly rate,' said he, smiling. 'The night mail from the north, which changes horses at Dwolding, passes within five miles of this spot, and will be due at a certain cross-road in about an hour and a quarter. If Jacob were to go with you across the moor, and put you into the old coach-road, you could find your way, I suppose, to where it joins the new one?'

'Easily—gladly.'

He smiled again, rang the bell, gave the old servant his directions, and, taking a bottle of whisky and a wineglass from the cupboard in which he kept his chemicals, said:

'The snow lies deep, and it will be difficult walking tonight on the moor. A glass of usquebaugh before you start?'

I would have declined the spirit, but he pressed it on me, and I drank it. It went down my throat like liquid flame, and almost took my breath away.

'It is strong,' he said; 'but it will help to keep out the cold. And now you have no moments to spare. Good night!'

I thanked him for his hospitality, and would have shaken hands, but that he had turned away before I could finish my sentence. In another minute I had traversed the hall, Jacob had locked the outer door behind me, and we were out on the wide white moor.

Although the wind had fallen, it was still bitterly cold. Not a star glimmered in the black vault overhead. Not a sound, save the rapid crunching of the snow beneath our feet, disturbed the heavy stillness of the night. Jacob, not too well pleased with his mission, shambled on before in sullen silence, his lantern in his hand, and his shadow at his feet. I followed, with my gun over my shoulder, as little inclined for conversation as himself. My thoughts were full of my late host. His voice yet rang in my ears. His eloquence yet held my imagination captive. I remember to this day, with surprise, how my over-excited brain retained whole sentences and parts of sentences, troops of brilliant images, and fragments of splendid reasoning, in the very words in which he had uttered them. Musing thus over what I had heard, and striving to recall a lost link here and there, I strode on at the heels of my guide, absorbed and unobservant. Presently—at the end, as it seemed to me, of only a few minutes—he came to a sudden halt, and said:

'Yon's your road. Keep the stone fence to your right hand, and you can't fail of the way.'

'This, then, is the old coach-road?'

'Ay, 'tis the old coach-road.'

'And how far do I go, before I reach the cross-roads?'

'Nigh upon three mile.'

I pulled out my purse, and he became more communicative.

'The road's a fair road enough,' said he, 'for foot passengers; but 'twas over steep and narrow for the northern traffic. You'll mind where the parapet's broken away, close again the sign-post. It's never been mended since the accident.'

'What accident?'

'Eh, the night mail pitched right over into the valley below—a gude fifty feet an' more—just at the worst bit o' road in the whole county.'

'Horrible! Were many lives lost?'

'All. Four were found dead, and t'other two died next morning.'

'How long is it since this happened?'

'Just nine year.'

'Near the sign-post, you say? I will bear it in mind. Good night.'

'Gude night, sir, and thankee.' Jacob pocketed his half-crown, made a faint pretence of touching his hat, and trudged back by the way he had come.

I watched the light of his lantern till it quite disappeared, and then turned to pursue my way alone. This was no longer matter of the slightest difficulty, for, despite the dead darkness overhead, the line of stone fence showed distinctly enough against the pale gleam of the snow. How silent it seemed now, with only my footsteps to listen to; how silent and how solitary! A strange disagreeable sense of loneliness stole over me. I walked faster. I hummed a fragment of a tune. I cast up enormous sums in my head, and accumulated them at compound interest. I did my best, in short, to forget the startling speculations to which I had but just been listening, and, to some extent, I succeeded.

Meanwhile the night air seemed to become colder and colder, and though I walked fast I found it impossible to keep myself warm. My feet were like ice. I lost sensation in my hands, and grasped my gun mechanically. I even breathed with difficulty, as though, instead of traversing a quiet north country highway, I were scaling the uppermost heights of some gigantic Alp. This last symptom became presently so distressing, that I was forced to stop for a few minutes, and lean against the stone fence. As I did so, I chanced to look back up the road, and there, to my infinite relief, I saw a distant point of light, like the gleam of an approaching lantern. I at first concluded that Jacob had retraced his steps and followed me; but even as the conjecture presented itself, a second light flashed into sight—a light evidently parallel with the first, and approaching at the same rate of motion. It needed no second thought to show me that these must be the carriage-lamps of some private vehicle, though it seemed strange that any private vehicle should take a road professedly disused and dangerous.

There could be no doubt, however, of the fact, for the lamps grew larger and brighter every moment, and I even fancied I could already see the dark outline of the carriage between them. It was coming up very fast, and quite noiselessly, the snow being nearly a foot deep under the wheels.

And now the body of the vehicle became distinctly visible behind the lamps. It looked strangely lofty. A sudden suspicion flashed upon me. Was it possible that I had passed the cross-roads in the dark without observing the sign-post, and could this be the very coach which I had come to meet?

No need to ask myself that question a second time, for here it came round the bend of the road, guard and driver, one outside passenger, and four steaming greys, all wrapped in a soft haze of light, through which the lamps blazed out, like a pair of fiery meteors.

I jumped forward, waved my hat, and shouted. The mail came down at full speed, and passed me. For a moment I feared that I had not been seen or heard, but it was only for a moment. The coachman pulled up; the guard, muffled to the eyes in capes and comforters, and apparently sound asleep in the rumble, neither answered my hail nor made the slightest effort to dismount; the outside passenger did not even turn his head. I opened the door for myself, and looked in. There were but three travellers inside, so I stepped in, shut the door, slipped into the vacant corner, and congratulated myself on my good fortune.

The atmosphere of the coach seemed, if possible, colder than that of the outer air, and was pervaded by a singularly damp and disagreeable smell. I looked round at my fellow-passengers. They were all three, men, and all silent. They did not seem to be asleep, but each leaned back in his corner of the vehicle, as if absorbed in his own reflections. I attempted to open a conversation.

'How intensely cold it is tonight,' I said, addressing my opposite neighbour.

He lifted his head, looked at me, but made no reply.

'The winter,' I added, 'seems to have begun in earnest.'

Although the corner in which he sat was so dim that I could distinguish none of his features very clearly, I saw that his eyes were still turned full upon me. And yet he answered never a word.

At any other time I should have felt, and perhaps expressed, some annoyance, but at the moment I felt too ill to do either. The icy coldness of the night air had struck a chill to my very marrow, and the strange smell inside the coach was affecting me with an intolerable nausea. I shivered from head to foot, and, turning to my left-hand neighbour, asked if he had any objection to an open window?

He neither spoke nor stirred.

I repeated the question somewhat more loudly, but with the same result. Then I lost patience, and let the sash down. As I did so the leather strap broke in my hand, and I observed that the glass was covered with a thick coat of mildew, the accumulation, apparently, of years. My attention being thus drawn to the condition of the coach, I examined it more narrowly, and saw by the uncertain light of the outer lamps that it was in the last stage of dilapidation. Every part of it was not only out of repair, but in a condition of decay. The sashes splintered at a touch. The leather fittings were crusted over with mould, and literally rotting from the woodwork. The floor was almost breaking away beneath my feet. The whole machine, in short, was foul with damp, and had evidently been dragged from some outhouse in which it had been mouldering away for years, to do another day or two of duty on the road.

I turned to the third passenger, whom I had not yet addressed, and hazarded one more remark.

'This coach,' I said, 'is in a deplorable condition. The regular mail, I suppose, is under repair?'

He moved his head slowly, and looked me in the face, without speaking a word. I shall never forget that look while I live. I turned cold at heart under it. I turn cold at heart even now when I recall it. His eyes glowed with a fiery unnatural lustre. His face was livid as the face of a corpse. His bloodless lips were drawn back as if in the agony of death, and showed the gleaming teeth between.

The words that I was about to utter died upon my lips, and a strange horror—a dreadful horror—came upon me. My sight had by this time become used to the gloom of the coach, and I could see with tolerable distinctness. I turned to my opposite neighbour. He, too, was looking at me, with the same startling pallor in his face, and the same stony glitter in his eyes. I passed my hand across my brow. I turned to the passenger on the seat beside my own, and saw—oh Heaven! how shall I describe what I saw? I saw that he was no living man—that none of them were living men, like myself! A pale phosphorescent light—the light of putrefaction—played upon their awful faces; upon their hair, dank with the dews of the grave; upon their clothes, earth-stained and dropping to pieces; upon their hands, which were as the hands of corpses long buried. Only their eyes, their terrible eyes, were living; and those eyes were all turned menacingly upon me!

A shriek of terror, a wild unintelligible cry for help and mercy, burst from my lips as I flung myself against the door, and strove in vain to open it.

In that single instant, brief and vivid as a landscape beheld in the flash of summer lightning, I saw the moon shining down through a rift of stormy cloud—the ghastly sign-post rearing its warning finger by the wayside—the broken parapet—the plunging horses—the black gulf below. Then, the coach reeled like a ship at sea. Then, came a mighty crash—a sense of crushing pain—and then, darkness.

It seemed as if years had gone by when I awoke one morning from a deep sleep, and found my wife watching by my bedside. I will pass over the scene that ensued, and give you, in half a dozen words, the tale she told me with tears of thanksgiving. I had fallen over a precipice, close against the junction of the old coach-road and the new, and had only been saved from certain death by lighting upon a deep snowdrift that had accumulated at the foot of the rock beneath. In this snowdrift I was discovered at daybreak, by a couple of shepherds, who carried me to the nearest shelter, and brought a surgeon to my aid. The surgeon found me in a state of raving delirium, with a broken arm and a compound fracture of the skull. The letters in my pocket-book showed my name and address; my wife was summoned to nurse me; and, thanks to youth and a fine constitution, I came out of danger at last. The place of my fall, I need scarcely say, was precisely that at which a frightful accident had happened to the north mail nine years before.

I never told my wife the fearful events which I have just related to you. I told the surgeon who attended me; but he treated the whole adventure as a mere dream born of the fever in my brain. We discussed the question over and over again, until we found that we could discuss it with temper no longer, and then we dropped it. Others may form what conclusions they please—I *know* that twenty years ago I was the fourth inside passenger in that Phantom Coach.

To Be Taken with a Grain of Salt

CHARLES DICKENS

I HAVE ALWAYS noticed a prevalent want of courage, even among persons of superior intelligence and culture, as to imparting their own psychological experiences when those have been of a strange sort. Almost all men are afraid that what they could relate in such wise would find no parallel or response in a listener's internal life, and might be suspected or laughed at. A truthful traveller who should have seen some extraordinary creature in the likeness of a sea-serpent, would have no fear of mentioning it; but the same traveller having had some singular presentiment, impulse, vagary of thought, vision (so-called), dream, or other remarkable mental impression, would hesitate considerably before he would own to it. To this reticence I attribute much of the obscurity in which such subjects are involved. We do not habitually communicate our experiences of these subjective things, as we do our experiences of objective creation. The consequence is, that the general stock of experience in this regard appears exceptional, and really is so, in respect of being miserably imperfect.

In what I am going to relate I have no intention of setting up, opposing, or supporting, any theory whatever. I know the history of the Bookseller of Berlin, I have studied the case of the wife of a late Astronomer Royal as related by Sir David Brewster, and I have followed the minutest details of a much more remarkable case of Spectral Illusion occurring within my private circle of friends. It may be necessary to state as to this last that the sufferer (a lady) was in no degree, however distant, related to me. A mistaken assumption on that head, might suggest an explanation of a part of my own case—but only a part—which would be wholly without foundation. It cannot be referred to my inheritance of any developed peculiarity, nor had I ever before any at all similar experience, nor have I ever had any at all similar experience since.

It does not signify how many years ago, or how few, a certain Murder was committed in England, which attracted great attention. We hear more than enough of Murderers as they rise in succession to their atrocious eminence, and I would bury the memory of this particular brute, if I could, as his body was buried, in Newgate Jail. I purposely abstain from giving any direct clue to the criminal's individuality.

When the murder was first discovered, no suspicion fell—or I ought rather to say, for I cannot be too precise in my facts, it was nowhere publicly hinted that any suspicion fell—on the man who was afterwards brought to trial. As no reference was at that time made to him in the newspapers, it is obviously impossible that any description of him can at that time have been given in the newspapers. It is essential that this fact be remembered.

Unfolding at breakfast my morning paper, containing the account of that first discovery, I found it to be deeply interesting, and I read it with close attention. I read it twice, if not three times. The discovery had been made in a bedroom, and, when I laid down the paper, I was aware of a flash—rush—flow—I do not know what to call it—no word I can find is satisfactorily descriptive—in which I seemed to see that bedroom passing through my room, like a picture impossibly painted on a running river. Though almost instantaneous in its passing, it was perfectly clear; so clear that I distinctly, and with a sense of relief, observed the absence of the dead body from the bed.

It was in no romantic place that I had this curious sensation, but in chambers in Piccadilly, very near to the corner of Saint James's Street. It was entirely new to me. I was in my easy-chair at the moment, and the sensation was accompanied with a peculiar shiver which started the chair from its position. (But it is to be noted that the chair ran easily on castors.) I went to one of the windows (there are two in the room, and the room is on the second floor) to refresh my eyes with the moving objects down in Piccadilly. It was a bright autumn morning, and the street was sparkling and cheerful. The wind was high. As I looked out, it brought down from the Park a quantity of fallen leaves, which a gust took, and whirled into a spiral pillar. As the pillar fell and the leaves dispersed, I saw two men on the opposite side of the way, going from West to East. They were one behind the other. The foremost man often looked back over his shoulder. The second man followed him, at a distance of some thirty paces, with his right hand menacingly raised. First, the singularity and steadiness of this threatening gesture in so public a thoroughfare, attracted my attention; and next, the more remarkable circumstance that nobody heeded it. Both men threaded their way among the other passengers, with a smoothness hardly consistent even with the action of walking on a pavement, and no single creature that I could see, gave them place, touched them, or looked after them. In passing before my windows, they both stared up at me. I saw their two faces very distinctly, and I knew that I could recognize them anywhere. Not that I had consciously noticed anything very remarkable in either face, except that the man who went first had an unusually lowering appearance, and that the face of the man who followed him was of the colour of impure wax.

I am a bachelor, and my valet and his wife constitute my whole establishment. My occupation is in a certain Branch Bank, and I wish that my duties as head of a Department were as light as they are popularly supposed to be. They kept me in town that autumn, when I stood in need of a change. I was not ill, but I was not well. My reader is to make the most that can be reasonably made of my feeling jaded, having a depressing sense upon me of a monotonous life, and being 'slightly dyspeptic'. I am assured by my renowned doctor that my real state of health at that time justifies no stronger description, and I quote his own from his written answer to my request for it.

As the circumstances of the Murder, gradually unravelling, took stronger and stronger possession of the public mind, I kept them away from mine, by knowing as little about them as was possible in the midst of the universal excitement. But I knew that a verdict of Wilful Murder had been found against the suspected Murderer, and that he had been committed to Newgate for trial. I also knew that his trial had been postponed over one Sessions of the Central Criminal Court, on the ground of general prejudice and want of time for the preparation of the defence. I may further have known, but I believe I did not, when, or about when, the Sessions to which his trial stood postponed would come on.

My sitting-room, bedroom, and dressing-room, are all on one floor. With the last, there is no communication but through the bedroom. True, there is a door in it, once communicating with the staircase; but a part of the fitting of my bath has been—and had then been for some years—fixed across it. At the same period, and as a part of the same arrangement, the door had been nailed up and canvassed over.

I was standing in my bedroom late one night, giving some directions to my servant before he went to bed. My face was towards the only available door of communication with the dressing-room, and it was closed. My servant's back was towards that door. While I was speaking to him I saw it open, and a man look in, who very earnestly and mysteriously beckoned to me. That man was the man who had gone second of the two along Piccadilly, and whose face was of the colour of impure wax.

The figure, having beckoned, drew back and closed the door. With no longer pause than was made by my crossing the bedroom, I opened the dressing-room door, and looked in. I had a lighted candle already in my hand. I felt no inward expectation of seeing the figure in the dressing-room, and I did not see it there.

Conscious that my servant stood amazed, I turned round to him, and said: 'Derrick, could you believe that in my cool senses I fancied I saw a——' As I there laid my hand upon his breast, with a sudden start he trembled violently, and said, 'O Lord yes sir! A dead man beckoning!'

Now, I do not believe that this John Derrick, my trusty and attached servant for more than twenty years, had any impression whatever of having seen any such figure, until I touched him. The change in him was so startling when I touched him, that I fully believe he derived his impression in some occult manner from me at that instant.

I bade John Derrick bring some brandy, and I gave him a dram, and was glad to take one myself. Of what had proceeded that night's phenomenon, I told him not a single word. Reflecting on it, I was absolutely certain that I had never seen that face before, except on the one occasion in Piccadilly. Comparing its expression when beckoning at the door, with its expression when it had stared up at me as I stood at my window, I came to the conclusion that on the first occasion it had sought to fasten itself upon my memory, and that on the second occasion it had made sure of being immediately remembered.

I was not very comfortable that night, though I felt a certainty, difficult to explain, that the figure would not return. At daylight, I fell into a heavy sleep, from which I was awakened by John Derrick's coming to my bedside with a paper in his hand.

This paper, it appeared, had been the subject of an altercation at the door between its bearer and my servant. It was a summons to me to serve upon a Jury at the forthcoming Sessions of the Central Criminal Court at the Old Bailey. I had never before been summoned on such a Jury, as John Derrick well knew. He believed—I am not certain at this hour whether with reason or otherwise—that that class of Jurors were customarily chosen on a lower qualification than mine, and he had at first refused to accept the summons. The man who served it had taken the matter very coolly. He had said that my attendance or non-attendance was nothing to him; there the summons was; and I should deal with it at my own peril, and not at his.

For a day or two I was undecided whether to respond to this call, or take no notice of it. I was not conscious of the slightest mysterious bias, influence, or attraction, one way or other. Of that I am as strictly sure as of every other statement that I make here. Ultimately I decided, as a break in the monotony of my life, that I would go.

The appointed morning was a raw morning in the month of November. There was a dense brown fog in Piccadilly, and it became positively black and in the last degree oppressive East of Temple Bar. I found the passages and staircases of the Court House flaringly lighted with gas, and the Court itself similarly illuminated. I *think* that until I was conducted by officers into the Old Court and saw its crowded state, I did not know that the Murderer was to be tried that day. I *think* that until I was so helped into the Old Court with considerable difficulty, I did not know into which of the two Courts sitting, my summons would take me. But this must not be received as a positive assertion, for I am not completely satisfied in my mind on either point.

I took my seat in the place appropriated to Jurors in waiting, and I looked about the Court as well as I could through the cloud of fog and breath that was heavy in it. I noticed the black vapour hanging like a murky curtain outside the great windows, and I noticed the stifled sound of wheels on the straw or tan that was littered in the street; also, the hum of the people gathered there, which a shrill whistle, or a louder song or hail than the rest, occasionally pierced. Soon afterwards the Judges, two in number, entered and took their seats. The buzz in the Court was awfully hushed. The direction was given to put the Murderer to the bar. He appeared there. And in that same instant I recognized in him, the first of the two men who had gone down Piccadilly.

If my name had been called then, I doubt if I could have answered to it audibly. But it was called about sixth or eighth in the panel, and I was by that time able to say 'Here!' Now, observe. As I stepped into the box, the prisoner, who had been looking on attentively but with no sign of concern, became violently agitated, and beckoned to his attorney. The prisoner's wish to challenge me was so manifest, that it occasioned a pause, during which the attorney, with his hand upon the dock, whispered with his client, and shook his head. I afterwards had it from that gentleman, that the prisoner's first affrighted words to him were, 'At all hazards challenge that man!' But, that as he would give no reason for it, and admitted that he had not even known my name until he heard it called and I appeared, it was not done.

Both on the ground already explained, that I wish to avoid reviving the unwholesome memory of that Murderer, and also because a detailed account of his long trial is by no means indispensable to my narrative, I shall confine myself closely to such incidents in the ten days and nights during which we, the Jury, were kept together, as directly bear on my own curious personal experience. It is in that, and not in the Murderer, that I seek to interest my reader. It is to that, and not to a page of the Newgate Calendar, that I beg attention.

I was chosen Foreman of the Jury. On the second morning of the trial, after evidence had been taken for two hours (I heard the church clocks strike), happening to cast my eyes over my brother-jurymen, I found an inexplicable difficulty in counting them. I counted them several times, yet always with the same difficulty. In short, I made them one too many.

I touched the brother-juryman whose place was next to me, and I whispered to him, 'Oblige me by counting us.' He looked surprised by the request, but turned his head and counted. 'Why,' says he, suddenly, 'We are Thirt——; but no, it's not possible. No. We are twelve.'

According to my counting that day, we were always right in detail, but in the gross we were always one too many. There was no appearance—no figure—to account for it; but I had now an inward foreshadowing of the figure that was surely coming.

The Jury were housed at the London Tavern. We all slept in one large room on separate tables, and we were constantly in the charge and under the eye of the officer sworn to hold us in safe-keeping. I see no reason for suppressing the real name of that officer. He was intelligent, highly polite, and obliging, and (I was glad to hear) much respected in the City. He had an agreeable presence, good eyes, enviable black whiskers, and a fine sonorous voice. His name was Mr Harker.

When we turned into our twelve beds at night, Mr Harker's bed was drawn across the door. On the night of the second day, not being disposed to lie down, and seeing Mr Harker sitting on his bed, I went and sat beside him, and offered him a pinch of snuff. As Mr Harker's hand touched mine in taking it from my box, a peculiar shiver crossed him, and he said: 'Who is this!'

Following Mr Harker's eyes and looking along the room, I saw again the figure I expected—the second of the two men who had gone down Piccadilly. I rose, and advanced a few steps; then stopped, and looked round at Mr Harker. He was quite unconcerned, laughed, and said in a pleasant way, 'I thought for a moment we had a thirteenth juryman, without a bed. But I see it is the moonlight.'

Making no revelation to Mr Harker, but inviting him to take a walk with me to the end of the room, I watched what the figure did. It stood for a few moments by the bedside of each of my eleven brother-jurymen, close to the pillow. It always went to the right-hand side of the bed, and always passed out crossing the foot of the next bed. It seemed from the action of the head, merely to look down pensively at each recumbent figure. It took no notice of me, or of my bed, which was that nearest to Mr Harker's. It seemed to go out where the moonlight came in, through a high window, as by an aërial flight of stairs.

Next morning at breakfast, it appeared that everybody present had dreamed of the murdered man last night, except myself and Mr Harker.

I now felt as convinced that the second man who had gone down Piccadilly was the murdered man (so to speak), as if it had been borne into my comprehension by his immediate testimony. But even this took place, and in a manner for which I was not at all prepared.

On the fifth day of the trial, when the case for the prosecution was drawing to a close, a miniature of the murdered man, missing from his bedroom upon the discovery of the deed, and afterwards found in a hiding-place where the Murderer had been seen digging, was put in evidence. Having been identified by the witness under examination, it was handed up to the Bench, and thence handed down to be inspected by the Jury. As an officer in a black gown was making his way with it across to me, the figure of the second man who had gone down Piccadilly, impetuously started from the crowd, caught the miniature from the officer, and gave it to me with its own hands, at the same time saying in a low and hollow tone—before I saw the miniature, which was in a locket—'I was younger then, and my face was not then drained of blood.' It also came between me and the brother-juryman to whom I would have given the miniature, and between him and the brother-juryman to whom he would have given it, and so passed it on through the whole of our number, and back into my possession. Not one of them, however, detected this.

At table, and generally when we were shut up together in Mr Harker's custody, we had from the first naturally discussed the day's proceedings a good deal. On that fifth day, the case for the prosecution being closed, and we having that side of the question in a completed shape before us, our discussion was more animated and serious. Among our number was a vestryman—the densest idiot I have ever seen at large—who met the plainest evidence with the most preposterous objections, and who was sided with by two flabby parochial parasites; all the three empanelled from a district so delivered over to Fever that they ought to have been upon their own trial, for five hundred Murders. When these mischievous blockheads were at their loudest, which was towards midnight while some of us were already preparing for bed, I again saw the murdered man. He stood grimly behind them, beckoning to me. On my going towards them and striking into the conversation, he immediately retired. This was the beginning of a separate series of appearances, confined to that long room in which we were confined. Whenever a knot of my brother jurymen laid their heads together, I saw the head of the murdered man among theirs. Whenever their comparison of notes was going against him, he would solemnly and irresistibly beckon to me.

It will be borne in mind that down to the production of the miniature on the fifth day of the trial, I had never seen the Appearance in Court. Three changes occurred, now that we entered on the case for the defence. Two of them I will mention together, first. The figure was now in Court continually, and it never there addressed itself to me, but always to the person who was speaking at the time. For instance. The throat of the

murdered man had been cut straight across. In the opening speech for
the defence, it was suggested that the deceased might have cut his own
throat. At that very moment, the figure with its throat in the dreadful
condition referred to (this it had concealed before) stood at the speaker's
elbow, motioning across and across its windpipe, now with the right
hand, now with the left, vigorously suggesting to the speaker himself, the
impossibility of such a wound having been self-inflicted by either hand.
For another instance. A witness to character, a woman, deposed to the
prisoner's being the most amiable of mankind. The figure at that instant
stood on the floor before her, looking her full in the face, and pointing
out the prisoner's evil countenance with an extended arm and an out-
stretched finger.

The third change now to be added, impressed me strongly, as the most
marked and striking of all. I do not theorize upon it; I accurately state it,
and there leave it. Although the Appearance was not itself perceived by
those whom it addressed, its coming close to such persons was invariably
attended by some trepidation or disturbance on their part. It seemed to
me as if it were prevented by laws to which I was not amenable, from fully
revealing itself to others, and yet as if it could, invisibly, dumbly and
darkly, overshadow their minds. When the leading counsel for the defence suggested that hypothesis of suicide and the figure stood at the
learned gentleman's elbow, frightfully sawing at its severed throat, it is
undeniable that the counsel faltered in his speech, lost for a few seconds
the thread of his ingenious discourse, wiped his forehead with his hand-
kerchief, and turned extremely pale. When the witness to character was
confronted by the Appearance, her eyes most certainly did follow the
direction of its pointed finger, and rest in great hesitation and trouble
upon the prisoner's face. Two additional illustrations will suffice. On the
eighth day of the trial, after the pause which was every day made early in
the afternoon for a few minutes' rest and refreshment, I came back into
Court with the rest of the Jury, some little time before the return of the
Judges. Standing up in the box and looking about me, I thought the
figure was not there, until, chancing to raise my eyes to the gallery, I saw
it bending forward and leaning over a very decent woman, as if to assure
itself whether the Judges had resumed their seats or not. Immediately
afterwards, that woman screamed, fainted, and was carried out. So with
the venerable, sagacious, and patient Judge who conducted the trial.
When the case was over, and he settled himself and his papers to sum up,
the murdered man entering by the Judges' door, advanced to his Lordship's desk, and looked eagerly over his shoulder at the pages of his notes
which he was turning. A change came over his Lordship's face; his hand
stopped; the peculiar shiver that I knew so well, passed over him; he

faltered, 'Excuse me gentlemen, for a few moments. I am somewhat oppressed by the vitiated air;' and did not recover until he had drunk a glass of water.

Through all the monotony of six of those interminable ten days—the same Judges and others on the bench, the same Murderer in the dock, the same lawyers at the table, the same tones of question and answer rising to the roof of the court, the same scratching of the Judge's pen, the same ushers going in and out, the same lights kindled at the same hour when there had been any natural light of day, the same foggy curtain outside the great windows when it was foggy, the same rain pattering and dripping when it was rainy, the same footmarks of turnkeys and prisoner day after day on the same sawdust, the same keys locking and unlocking the same heavy doors—through all the wearisome monotony which made me feel as if I had been Foreman of the Jury for a vast period of time, and Piccadilly had flourished coevally with Babylon, the murdered man never lost one trace of his distinctness in my eyes, nor was he at any moment less distinct than anybody else. I must not omit, as a matter of fact, that I never once saw the Appearance which I call by the name of the murdered man, look at the Murderer. Again and again I wondered, 'Why does he not?' But he never did.

Nor did he look at me, after the production of the miniature, until the last closing minutes of the trial arrived. We retired to consider, at seven minutes before ten at night. The idiotic vestryman and his two parochial parasites gave us so much trouble, that we twice returned into Court, to beg to have certain extracts from the Judge's notes reread. Nine of us had not the smallest doubt about those passages, neither, I believe, had any one in Court; the dunder-headed triumvirate however, having no idea but obstruction, disputed them for that very reason. At length we prevailed, and finally the Jury returned into Court at ten minutes past twelve.

The murdered man at that time stood directly opposite the Jury-box, on the other side of the Court. As I took my place, his eyes rested on me, with great attention; he seemed satisfied, and slowly shook a great grey veil, which he carried on his arm for the first time, over his head and whole form. As I gave in our verdict 'Guilty', the veil collapsed, all was gone, and his place was empty.

The Murderer being asked by the Judge, according to usage, whether he had anything to say before sentence of Death should be passed upon him, indistinctly muttered something which was described in the leading newspapers of the following day as 'a few rambling, incoherent, and half-audible words, in which he was understood to complain that he had not had a fair trial because the Foreman of the Jury was prepossessed against him'. The remarkable declaration that he really made, was this: '*My Lord, I knew I was a doomed man when the Foreman of my Jury came into the box. My Lord, I knew he would never let me off, because, before I was taken, he somehow got to my bedside in the night, woke me, and put a rope round my neck.*'

Dickon the Devil

J. S. LeFanu

ABOUT THIRTY YEARS ago I was selected by two rich old maids to visit a property in that part of Lancashire which lies near the famous forest of Pendle, with which Mr Ainsworth's 'Lancashire Witches' has made us so pleasantly familiar. My business was to make partition of a small property, including a house and demesne, to which they had a long time before succeeded as co-heiresses.

The last forty miles of my journey I was obliged to post, chiefly by cross-roads, little known, and less frequented, and presenting scenery often extremely interesting and pretty. The picturesqueness of the landscape was enhanced by the season, the beginning of September, at which I was travelling.

I had never been in this part of the world before; I am told it is now a great deal less wild, and, consequently, less beautiful.

At the inn where I had stopped for a relay of horses and some dinner—for it was then past five o'clock—I found the host, a hale old fellow of five-and-sixty, as he told me, a man of easy and garrulous benevolence, willing to accommodate his guests with any amount of talk, which the slightest tap sufficed to set flowing, on any subject you pleased.

I was curious to learn something about Barwyke, which was the name of the demesne and house I was going to. As there was no inn within some miles of it, I had written to the steward to put me up there, the best way he could, for a night.

The host of the 'Three Nuns,' which was the sign under which he entertained wayfarers, had not a great deal to tell. It was twenty years, or more, since old Squire Bowes died, and no one had lived in the Hall ever since, except the gardener and his wife.

'Tom Wyndsour will be as old a man as myself; but he's a bit taller, and not so much in flesh, quite,' said the fat innkeeper.

'But there were stories about the house,' I repeated, 'that they said, prevented tenants from coming into it?'

'Old wives' tales; many years ago, that will be, sir; I forget 'em; I forget 'em all. Oh yes, there always will be, when a house is left so; foolish folk will always be talkin'; but I hadn't heard a word about it this twenty year.'

It was vain trying to pump him; the old landlord of the 'Three Nuns,' for some reason, did not choose to tell tales of Barwyke Hall, if he really did, as I suspected, remember them.

23

I paid my reckoning, and resumed my journey, well pleased with the good cheer of that old-world inn, but a little disappointed.

We had been driving for more than an hour, when we began to cross a wild common; and I knew that, this passed, a quarter of an hour would bring me to the door of Barwyke Hall.

The peat and furze were pretty soon left behind; we were again in the wooded scenery that I enjoyed so much, so entirely natural and pretty, and so little disturbed by traffic of any kind. I was looking from the chaise-window, and soon detected the object of which, for some time, my eye had been in search. Barwyke Hall was a large, quaint house, of that cage-work fashion known as 'black-and-white,' in which the bars and angles of an oak framework contrast, black as ebony, with the white plaster that overspreads the masonry built into its interstices. This steep-roofed Elizabethan house stood in the midst of park-like grounds of no great extent, but rendered imposing by the noble stature of the old trees that now cast their lengthening shadows eastward over the sward, from the declining sun.

The park-wall was grey with age, and in many places laden with ivy. In deep grey shadow, that contrasted with the dim fires of evening reflected on the foliage above it, in a gentle hollow, stretched a lake that looked cold and black, and seemed, as it were, to skulk from observation with a guilty knowledge.

I had forgot that there was a lake at Barwyke; but the moment this caught my eye, like the cold polish of a snake in the shadow, my instinct seemed to recognize something dangerous, and I knew that the lake was connected, I could not remember how, with the story I had heard of this place in my boyhood.

I drove up a grass-grown avenue, under the boughs of these noble trees, whose foliage, dyed in autumnal red and yellow, returned the beams of the western sun gorgeously.

We drew up at the door. I got out, and had a good look at the front of the house; it was a large and melancholy mansion, with signs of long neglect upon it; great wooden shutters, in the old fashion, were barred, outside, across the windows; grass, and even nettles, were growing thick on the courtyard, and a thin moss streaked the timber beams; the plaster was discoloured by time and weather, and bore great russet and yellow stains. The gloom was increased by several grand old trees that crowded close about the house.

I mounted the steps, and looked round; the dark lake lay near me now, a little to the left. It was not large; it may have covered some ten or twelve acres; but it added to the melancholy of the scene. Near the centre of it was a small island, with two old ash trees, leaning toward each other, their pensive images reflected in the stirless water. The only cheery influence in this scene of antiquity, solitude, and neglect was that the house and landscape were warmed with the ruddy western beams. I knocked, and my summons resounded hollow and ungenial in my ear; and the bell, from far away, returned a deep-mouthed and surly ring, as if it resented being roused from a score years' slumber.

A light-limbed, jolly-looking old fellow, in a barracan jacket and gaiters, with a smile of welcome, and a very sharp, red nose, that seemed to promise good cheer, opened the door with a promptitude that indicated a hospitable expectation of my arrival.

There was but little light in the hall, and that little lost itself in darkness in the background. It was very spacious and lofty, with a gallery running round it, which, when the door was open, was visible at two or three points. Almost in the dark my new acquaintance led me across this wide hall into the room destined for my reception. It was spacious, and wainscoted up to the ceiling. The furniture of this capacious chamber was old-fashioned and clumsy. There were curtains still to the windows, and a piece of Turkey carpet lay upon the floor; those windows were two in number, looking out, through the trunks of the trees close to the house, upon the lake. It needed all the fire, and all the pleasant associations of my entertainer's red nose, to light up this melancholy chamber. A door at its farther end admitted to the room that was prepared for my sleeping apartment. It was wainscoted, like the other. It had a four-post bed, with heavy tapestry curtains, and in other respects was furnished in the same old-world and ponderous style as the other room. Its window, like those of that apartment, looked out upon the lake.

Sombre and sad as these rooms were, they were yet scrupulously clean. I had nothing to complain of; but the effect was rather dispiriting. Having given some directions about supper—a pleasant incident to look forward to—and made a rapid toilet, I called on my friend with the gaiters and red nose (Tom Wyndsour) whose occupation was that of a 'bailiff,' or under-steward, of the property, to accompany me, as we had still an hour or so of sun and twilight, in a walk over the grounds.

It was a sweet autumn evening, and my guide, a hardy old fellow, strode at a pace that tasked me to keep up with.

Among clumps of trees at the northern boundary of the demesne we lighted upon the little antique parish church. I was looking down upon it, from an eminence, and the park-wall interposed; but a little way down was a stile affording access to the road, and by this we approached the iron gate of the churchyard. I saw the church door open; the sexton was replacing his pick, shovel, and spade, with which he had just been digging a grave in the churchyard, in their little repository under the stone stair of the tower. He was a polite, shrewd little hunchback, who was very happy to show me over the church. Among the monuments was one that interested me; it was erected to commemorate the very Squire Bowes from whom my two old maids had inherited the house and estate of Barwyke. It spoke of him in terms of grandiloquent eulogy, and informed the Christian reader that he had died, in the bosom of the Church of England, at the age of seventy-one.

I read this inscription by the parting beams of the setting sun, which disappeared behind the horizon just as we passed out from under the porch.

'Twenty years since the Squire died,' said I, reflecting as I loitered still in the churchyard.

'Ay, sir; 'twill be twenty year the ninth o' last month.'

'And a very good old gentleman?'

'Good-natured enough, and an easy gentleman he was, sir; I don't think while he lived he ever hurt a fly,' acquiesced Tom Wyndsour. 'It ain't always easy sayin' what's in 'em though, and what they may take or turn to afterwards; and some o' them sort, I think, goes mad.'

'You don't think he was out of his mind?' I asked.

'He? La! no; not he, sir; a bit lazy, mayhap, like other old fellows; but a knew devilish well what he was about.'

Tom Wyndsour's account was a little enigmatical; but, like old Squire Bowes, I was 'a bit lazy' that evening, and asked no more questions about him.

We got over the stile upon the narrow road that skirts the churchyard. It is overhung by elms more than a hundred years old, and in the twilight, which now prevailed, was growing very dark. As side-by-side we walked along this road, hemmed in by two loose stone-like walls, something running towards us in a zig-zag line passed us at a wild pace, with a sound like a frightened laugh or a shudder, and I saw, as it passed, that it was a human figure. I may confess now, that I was a little startled. The dress of this figure was, in part, white: I know I mistook it at first for a white horse coming down the road at a gallop. Tom Wyndsour turned about and looked after the retreating figure.

'He'll be on his travels to-night,' he said, in a low tone. 'Easy served with a bed, *that* lad be; six foot o' dry peat or heath, or a nook in a dry ditch. That lad hasn't slept once in a house this twenty year, and never will while grass grows.'

'Is he mad?' I asked.

'Something that way, sir; he's an idiot, an awpy; we call him "Dickon the devil," because the devil's almost the only word that's ever in his mouth.'

It struck me that this idiot was in some way connected with the story of old Squire Bowes.

'Queer things are told of him, I dare say?' I suggested.

'More or less, sir; more or less. Queer stories, some.'

'Twenty years since he slept in a house? That's about the time the Squire died,' I continued.

'So it will be, sir; and not very long after.'

'You must tell me all about that, Tom, to-night, when I can hear it comfortably, after supper.'

Tom did not seem to like my invitation; and looking straight before him as we trudged on, he said,

'You see, sir, the house has been quiet, and nout's been troubling folk inside the walls or out, all round the woods of Barwyke, this ten year, or more; and my old woman, down there, is clear against talking about such matters, and thinks it best—and so do I—to let sleepin' dogs be.'

He dropped his voice towards the close of the sentence, and nodded significantly.

We soon reached a point where he unlocked a wicket in the park wall, by which we entered the grounds of Barwyke once more.

The twilight deepening over the landscape, the huge and solemn trees, and the distant outline of the haunted house, exercised a sombre influence on me, which, together with the fatigue of a day of travel, and the brisk walk we had had, disinclined me to interrupt the silence in which my companion now indulged.

A certain air of comparative comfort, on our arrival, in great measure dissipated the gloom that was stealing over me. Although it was by no means a cold night, I was very glad to see some wood blazing in the grate; and a pair of candles aiding the light of the fire, made the room look cheerful. A small table, with a very white cloth, and preparations for supper, was also a very agreeable object.

I should have liked very well, under these influences, to have listened to Tom Wyndsour's story; but after supper I grew too sleepy to attempt to lead him to the subject; and after yawning for a time, I found there was no use in contending against my drowsiness, so I betook myself to my bedroom, and by ten o'clock was fast asleep.

What interruption I experienced that night I shall tell you presently. It was not much, but it was very odd.

By next night I had completed my work at Barwyke. From early morning till then I was so incessantly occupied and hard-worked, that I had not time to think over the singular occurrence to which I have just referred. Behold me, however, at length once more seated at my little supper-table, having ended a comfortable meal. It had been a sultry day, and I had thrown one of the large windows up as high as it would go. I was sitting near it, with my brandy and water at my elbow, looking out into the dark. There was no moon, and the trees that are grouped about the house make the darkness round it supernaturally profound on such nights.

'Tom,' said I, so soon as the jug of hot punch I had supplied him with began to exercise its genial and communicative influence; 'you must tell me who beside your wife and you and myself slept in the house last night.'

Tom, sitting near the door, set down his tumbler, and looked at me askance, while you might count seven, without speaking a word.

'Who else slept in the house?' he repeated, very deliberately. 'Not a living soul, sir;' and he looked hard at me, still evidently expecting something more.

'That is very odd,' I said returning his stare, and feeling really a little odd. 'You are sure you were not in my room last night?'

'Not till I came to call you, sir, this morning; I can make oath of that.'

'Well,' said I, 'there was some one there, I can make oath of that. I was so tired I could not make up my mind to get up; but I was waked by a sound that I thought was some one flinging down the two tin boxes in which my papers were locked up violently on the floor. I heard a slow step on the ground, and there was light in the room, although I remembered having put out my candle. I thought it must have been you, who had come in for my clothes, and upset the boxes by accident. Whoever it was, he went out and the light with him. I was about to settle again, when, the curtain being a little open at the foot of the bed, I saw a light on the wall opposite; such as a candle from outside would cast if the door were very cautiously opening. I started up in the bed, drew the side curtain, and saw that the door was opening, and admitting light from outside. It is close, you know, to the head of the bed. A hand was holding on the edge of the door and pushing it open; not a bit like yours; a very singular hand. Let me look at yours.'

He extended it for my inspection.

'Oh no; there's nothing wrong with your hand. This was differently shaped; fatter; and the middle finger was stunted, and shorter than the rest, looking as if it had once been broken, and the nail was crooked like a claw. I called out "Who's there?" and the light and the hand were withdrawn, and I saw and heard no more of my visitor.'

'So sure as you're a living man, that was him!' exclaimed Tom Wynd-sour, his very nose growing pale, and his eyes almost starting out of his head.

'Who?' I asked.

'Old Squire Bowes; 'twas *his* hand you saw; the Lord a' mercy on us!' answered Tom. 'The broken finger, and the nail bent like a hoop. Well for you, sir, he didn't come back when you called, that time. You came here about them Miss Dymocks' business, and he never meant they should have a foot o' ground in Barwyke; and he was making a will to give it away quite different, when death took him short. He never was uncivil to no one; but he couldn't abide them ladies. My mind misgave me when I heard 'twas about their business you were coming; and now you see how it is; he'll be at his old tricks again!'

With some pressure and a little more punch, I induced Tom Wyndsour to explain his mysterious allusions by recounting the occurrences which followed the old Squire's death.

'Squire Bowes of Barwyke died without making a will, as you know,' said Tom. 'And all the folk round were sorry; that is to say, sir, as sorry as folk will be for an old man that has seen a long tale of years, and has no right to grumble that death has knocked an hour too soon at his door. The Squire was well liked; he was never in a passion, or said a hard word; and he would not hurt a fly; and that made what happened after his decease the more surprising.

'The first thing these ladies did, when they got the property, was to buy stock for the park.

'It was not wise, in any case, to graze the land on their own account. But they little knew all they had to contend with.

'Before long something went wrong with the cattle; first one, and then another, took sick and died, and so on, till the loss began to grow heavy. Then, queer stories, little by little, began to be told. It was said, first by one, then by another, that Squire Bowes was seen, about evening time, walking, just as he used to do when he was alive, among the old trees, leaning on his stick; and, sometimes when he came up with the cattle, he would stop and lay his hand kindly like on the back of one of them; and that one was sure to fall sick next day, and die soon after.

'No one ever met him in the park, or in the woods, or ever saw him, except a good distance off. But they knew his gait and his figure well, and the clothes he used to wear; and they could tell the beast he laid his hand on by its colour—white, dun, or black; and that beast was sure to sicken and die. The neighbours grew shy of taking the path over the park; and no one liked to walk in the woods, or come inside the bounds of Barwyke: and the cattle went on sickening and dying as before.

'At that time there was one Thomas Pyke; he had been a groom to the old Squire; and he was in care of the place, and was the only one that used to sleep in the house.

'Tom was vexed, hearing these stories; which he did not believe the half

on 'em; and more especial as he could not get man or boy to herd the
cattle; all being afeared. So he wrote to Matlock in Derbyshire, for his
brother, Richard Pyke, a clever lad, and one that knew nout o' the story of
the old Squire walking.

'Dick came; and the cattle was better; folk said they could still see the
old Squire, sometimes, walking, as before, in openings of the wood, with
his stick in his hand; but he was shy of coming nigh the cattle, whatever
his reason might be, since Dickon Pyke came; and he used to stand a long
bit off, looking at them, with no more stir in him than a trunk o' one of
the old trees, for an hour at a time, till the shape melted away, little by
little, like the smoke of a fire that burns out.

'Tom Pyke and his brother Dickon, being the only living souls in the
house, lay in the big bed in the servants' room, the house being fast
barred and locked, one night in November.

'Tom was lying next the wall, and he told me, as wide awake as ever he
was at noonday. His brother Dickon lay outside, and was sound asleep.

'Well, as Tom lay thinking, with his eyes turned toward the door, it
opens slowly, and who should come in but old Squire Bowes, his face
lookin' as dead as he was in his coffin.

'Tom's very breath left his body; he could not take his eyes off him; and
he felt the hair rising up on his head.

'The Squire came to the side of the bed, and put his arms under
Dickon, and lifted the boy—in a dead sleep all the time—and carried
him out so, at the door.

'Such was the appearance, to Tom Pyke's eyes, and he was ready to
swear to it, anywhere.

'When this happened, the light, wherever it came from, all on a
sudden went out, and Tom could not see his own hand before him.

'More dead than alive, he lay till daylight.

'Sure enough his brother Dickon was gone. No sign of him could he
discover about the house; and with some trouble he got a couple of the
neighbours to help him to search the woods and grounds. Not a sign of
him anywhere.

'At last one of them thought of the island in the lake; the little boat was
moored to the old post at the water's edge. In they got, though with small
hope of finding him there. Find him, nevertheless, they did, sitting
under the big ash tree, quite out of his wits; and to all their questions he
answered nothing but one cry—"Bowes, the devil! See him; see him;
Bowes, the devil!" An idiot they found him; and so he will be till God sets
all things right. No one could ever get him to sleep under roof-tree more.
He wanders from house to house while daylight lasts; and no one cares to
lock the harmless creature in the workhouse. And folk would rather not

meet him after nightfall, for they think where he is there may be worse things near.'

A silence followed Tom's story. He and I were alone in that large room; I was sitting near the open window, looking into the dark night air. I fancied I saw something white move across it; and I heard a sound like low talking that swelled into a discordant shriek—'Hoo-oo-oo! Bowes, the devil! Over your shoulder. Hoo-oo-oo! ha! ha! ha!' I started up, and saw, by the light of the candle with which Tom strode to the window, the wild eyes and blighted face of the idiot, as, with a sudden change of mood, he drew off, whispering and tittering to himself, and holding up his long fingers, and looking at the tips like a 'hand of glory.'

Tom pulled down the window. The story and its epilogue were over. I confess I was rather glad when I heard the sound of the horses' hoofs on the court-yard, a few minutes later; and still gladder when, having bidden Tom a kind farewell, I had left the neglected house of Barwyke a mile behind me.

The Judge's House

BRAM STOKER

WHEN THE TIME for his examination drew near Malcolm Malcolmson made up his mind to go somewhere to read by himself. He feared the attractions of the seaside, and also he feared completely rural isolation, for of old he knew its charms, and so he determined to find some unpretentious little town where there would be nothing to distract him. He refrained from asking suggestions from any of his friends, for he argued that each would recommend some place of which he had knowledge, and where he had already acquaintances. As Malcolmson wished to avoid friends he had no wish to encumber himself with the attention of friends' friends, and so he determined to look out for a place for himself. He packed a portmanteau with some clothes and all the books he required, and then took ticket for the first name on the local time-table which he did not know.

When at the end of three hours' journey he alighted at Benchurch, he felt satisfied that he had so far obliterated his tracks as to be sure of having a peaceful opportunity of pursuing his studies. He went straight to the one inn which the sleepy little place contained, and put up for the night. Benchurch was a market town, and once in three weeks was crowded to excess, but for the remainder of the twenty-one days it was as attractive as a desert. Malcolmson looked around the day after his arrival to try to find quarters more isolated than even so quiet an inn as 'The Good Traveller' afforded. There was only one place which took his fancy, and it certainly satisfied his wildest ideas regarding quiet; in fact, quiet was not the proper word to apply to it—desolation was the only term conveying any suitable idea of its isolation. It was an old rambling, heavy-built house of the Jacobean style, with heavy gables and windows, unusually small, and set higher than was customary in such houses, and was surrounded with a high brick wall massively built. Indeed, on examination, it looked more like a fortified house than an ordinary dwelling. But all these things pleased Malcolmson. 'Here,' he thought, 'is the very spot I have been looking for, and if I can only get opportunity of using it I shall be happy.' His joy was increased when he realised beyond doubt that it was not at present inhabited.

From the post-office he got the name of the agent, who was rarely surprised at the application to rent a part of the old house. Mr Carnford, the local lawyer and agent, was a genial old gentleman, and frankly confessed his delight at anyone being willing to live in the house.

'To tell you the truth,' said he, 'I should be only too happy, on behalf of the owners, to let anyone have the house rent free for a term of years if only to accustom the people here to see it inhabited. It has been so long empty that some kind of absurd prejudice has grown up about it, and this can be best put down by its occupation—if only,' he added with a sly glance at Malcolmson, 'by a scholar like yourself, who wants it quiet for a time.'

Malcolmson thought it needless to ask the agent about the 'absurd prejudice'; he knew he would get more information, if he should require it, on that subject from other quarters. He paid his three months' rent, got a receipt, and the name of an old woman who would probably undertake to 'do' for him, and came away with the keys in his pocket. He then went to the landlady of the inn, who was a cheerful and most kindly person, and asked her advice as to such stores and provisions as he would be likely to require. She threw up her hands in amazement when he told her where he was going to settle himself.

'Not in the Judge's House!' she said, and grew pale as she spoke. He explained the locality of the house, saying that he did not know its name. When he had finished she answered:

'Aye, sure enough—sure enough the very place! It is the Judge's House sure enough.' He asked her to tell him about the place, why so called, and what there was against it. She told him that it was so called locally because it had been many years before—how long she could not say, as she was herself from another part of the country, but she thought it must have been a hundred years or more—the abode of a judge who was held in great terror on account of his harsh sentences and his hostility to prisoners at Assizes. As to what there was against the house itself she could not tell. She had often asked, but no one could inform her; but there was a general feeling that there was *something*, and for her own part she would not take all the money in Drinkwater's Bank and stay in the house an hour by herself. Then she apologised to Malcolmson for her disturbing talk.

'It is too bad of me, sir, and you—and a young gentleman, too—if you will pardon me saying it, going to live there all alone. If you were my boy—and you'll excuse me for saying it—you wouldn't sleep there a night, not if I had to go there myself and pull the big alarm bell that's on the roof!' The good creature was so manifestly in earnest, and was so kindly in her intentions, that Malcolmson, although amused, was touched. He told her kindly how much he appreciated her interest in him, and added:

'But, my dear Mrs Witham, indeed you need not be concerned about me! A man who is reading for the Mathematical Tripos has too much to think of to be disturbed by any of these mysterious "somethings", and his work is of too exact and prosaic a kind to allow of his having any corner in his mind for mysteries of any kind. Harmonical Progression, Permutations and Combinations, and Elliptic Functions have sufficient mysteries for me!' Mrs Witham kindly undertook to see after his commissions, and he went himself to look for the old woman who had been recommended to him. When he returned to the Judge's House with her, after an interval of a couple of hours, he found Mrs Witham herself waiting with several men and boys carrying parcels, and an upholsterer's man with a bed in a cart, for she said, though tables and chairs might be all very well, a bed that hadn't been aired for mayhap fifty years was not proper for young bones to lie on. She was evidently curious to see the inside of the house; and though manifestly so afraid of the 'somethings' that at the slightest sound she clutched on to Malcolmson, whom she never left for a moment, went over the whole place.

After his examination of the house, Malcolmson decided to take up his abode in the great dining-room, which was big enough to serve for all his requirements; and Mrs Witham, with the aid of the charwoman, Mrs Dempster, proceeded to arrange matters. When the hampers were brought in and unpacked, Malcolmson saw that with much kind forethought she had sent from her own kitchen sufficient provisions to last for a few days. Before going she expressed all sorts of kind wishes; and at the door turned and said:

'And perhaps, sir, as the room is big and draughty it might be well to have one of those big screens put round your bed at night—though, truth to tell, I would die myself if I were to be so shut in with all kinds of—of "things", that put their heads round the sides, or over the top, and look on me!' The image which she had called up was too much for her nerves, and she fled incontinently.

Mrs Dempster sniffed in a superior manner as the landlady disappeared, and remarked that for her own part she wasn't afraid of all the bogies in the kingdom.

'I'll tell you what it is, sir,' she said; 'bogies is all kinds and sorts of things—except bogies! Rats and mice, and beetles; and creaky doors, and loose slates, and broken panes, and stiff drawer handles, that stay out when you pull them and then fall down in the middle of the night. Look at the wainscot of the room! It is old—hundreds of years old! Do you think there's no rats and beetles there! And do you imagine, sir, that you won't see none of them! Rats is bogies, I tell you, and bogies is rats; and don't you get to think anything else!'

'Mrs Dempster,' said Malcolmson gravely, making her a polite bow, 'you know more than a Senior Wrangler! And let me say, that, as a mark of esteem for your indubitable soundness of head and heart, I shall, when I go, give you possession of this house, and let you stay here by yourself for the last two months of my tenancy, for four weeks will serve my purpose.'

'Thank you kindly, sir!' she answered, 'but I couldn't sleep away from home a night. I am in Greenhow's Charity, and if I slept a night away from my rooms I should lose all I have got to live on. The rules is very strict; and there's too many watching for a vacancy for me to run any risks in the matter. Only for that, sir, I'd gladly come here and attend on you altogether during your stay.'

'My good woman,' said Malcolmson hastily, 'I have come here on purpose to obtain solitude; and believe me that I am grateful to the late Greenhow for having so organised his admirable charity—whatever it is—that I am perforce denied the opportunity of suffering from such a form of temptation! Saint Anthony himself could not be more rigid on the point!'

The old woman laughed harshly. 'Ah, you young gentlemen,' she said, 'you don't fear for naught; and belike you'll get all the solitude you want here.' She set to work with her cleaning; and by nightfall, when Malcolmson returned from his walk—he always had one of his books to study as he walked—he found the room swept and tidied, a fire burning in the old hearth, the lamp lit, and the table spread for supper with Mrs Witham's excellent fare. 'This is comfort, indeed,' he said, as he rubbed his hands.

When he had finished his supper, and lifted the tray to the other end of the great oak dining-table, he got out his books again, put fresh wood on the fire, trimmed his lamp, and set himself down to a spell of real hard work. He went on without pause till about eleven o'clock, when he knocked off for a bit to fix his fire and lamp, and to make himself a cup of tea. He had always been a tea-drinker, and during his college life had sat late at work and had taken tea late. The rest was a great luxury to him, and he enjoyed it with a sense of delicious, voluptuous ease. The renewed fire leaped and sparkled, and threw quaint shadows through the great old room; and as he sipped his hot tea he revelled in the sense of isolation from his kind. Then it was that he began to notice for the first time what a noise the rats were making.

'Surely,' he thought, 'they cannot have been at it all the time I was reading. Had they been, I must have noticed it!' Presently, when the noise increased, he satisfied himself that it was really new. It was evident that at first the rats had been frightened at the presence of a stranger, and the light of fire and lamp; but that as the time went on they had grown bolder and were now disporting themselves as was their wont.

How busy they were! and hark to the strange noises! Up and down behind the old wainscot, over the ceiling and under the floor they raced, and gnawed, and scratched! Malcolmson smiled to himself as he recalled to mind the saying of Mrs Dempster, 'Bogies is rats, and rats is bogies!' The tea began to have its effect of intellectual and nervous stimulus, he saw with joy another long spell of work to be done before the night was past, and in the sense of security which it gave him, he allowed himself the luxury of a good look round the room. He took his lamp in one hand, and went all around, wondering that so quaint and beautiful an old house had been so long neglected. The carving of the oak on the panels of the wainscot was fine, and on and round the doors and windows it was beautiful and of rare merit. There were some old pictures on the walls, but they were coated so thick with dust and dirt that he could not distinguish any detail of them, though he held his lamp as high as he could over his head. Here and there as he went round he saw some crack or hole blocked for a moment by the face of a rat with its bright eyes glittering in the light, but in an instant it was gone, and a squeak and a scamper followed.

The thing that most struck him, however, was the rope of the great alarm bell on the roof, which hung down in a corner of the room on the right-hand side of the fireplace. He pulled up close to the hearth a great high-backed carved oak chair, and sat down to his last cup of tea. When this was done he made up the fire, and went back to his work, sitting at the corner of the table, having the fire to his left. For a while the rats disturbed him somewhat with their perpetual scampering, but he got accustomed to the noise as one does to the ticking of a clock or to the roar of moving water; and he became so immersed in his work that everything in the world, except the problem which he was trying to solve, passed away from him.

He suddenly looked up, his problem was still unsolved, and there was in the air that sense of the hour before the dawn, which is so dread to doubtful life. The noise of the rats had ceased. Indeed it seemed to him that it must have ceased but lately and that it was the sudden cessation which had disturbed him. The fire had fallen low, but still it threw out a deep red glow. As he looked he started in spite of his *sang froid*.

There on the great high-backed carved oak chair by the right side of the fireplace sat an enormous rat, steadily glaring at him with baleful eyes. He made a motion to it as though to hunt it away, but it did not stir. Then he made the motion of throwing something. Still it did not stir, but showed its great white teeth angrily, and its cruel eyes shone in the lamplight with an added vindictiveness.

Malcolmson felt amazed, and seizing the poker from the hearth ran at it to kill it. Before, however, he could strike it, the rat, with a squeak that sounded like the concentration of hate, jumped upon the floor, and, running up the rope of the alarm bell, disappeared in the darkness beyond the range of the green-shaded lamp. Instantly, strange to say, the noisy scampering of the rats in the wainscot began again.

By this time Malcolmson's mind was quite off the problem; and as a shrill cock-crow outside told him of the approach of morning, he went to bed and to sleep.

He slept so sound that he was not even waked by Mrs Dempster coming in to make up his room. It was only when she had tidied up the place and got his breakfast ready and tapped on the screen which closed in his bed that he woke. He was a little tired still after his night's hard work, but a strong cup of tea soon freshened him up, and, taking his book, he went out for his morning walk, bringing with him a few sandwiches lest he should not care to return till dinner time. He found a quiet walk between high elms some way outside the town, and here he spent the greater part of the day studying his Laplace. On his return he looked in to see Mrs Witham and to thank her for her kindness. When she saw him coming through the diamond-paned bay-window of her sanctum she came out to meet him and asked him in. She looked at him searchingly and shook her head as she said:

'You must not overdo it, sir. You are paler this morning than you should be. Too late hours and too hard work on the brain isn't good for any man! But tell me, sir, how did you pass the night? Well, I hope? But, my heart! sir, I was glad when Mrs Dempster told me this morning that you were all right and sleeping sound when she went in.'

'Oh, I was all right,' he answered, smiling, 'the "somethings" didn't worry me, as yet. Only the rats; and they had a circus, I tell you, all over the place. There was one wicked looking old devil that sat up on my own chair by the fire, and wouldn't go till I took the poker to him, and then he ran up the rope of the alarm bell and got to somewhere up the wall or the ceiling—I couldn't see where, it was so dark.'

'Mercy on us,' said Mrs Witham, 'an old devil, and sitting on a chair by the fireside! Take care, sir! take care! There's many a true word spoken in jest.'

'How do you mean? 'Pon my word I don't understand.'

'An old devil! The old devil, perhaps. There! sir, you. needn't laugh,' for Malcolmson had broken into a hearty peal. 'You young folks thinks it easy to laugh at things that makes older ones shudder. Never mind, sir! never mind! Please God, you'll laugh all the time. It's what I wish you myself!' and the good lady beamed all over in sympathy with his enjoyment, her fears gone for a moment.

'Oh, forgive me!' said Malcolmson presently. 'Don't think me rude; but the idea was too much for me—that the old devil himself was on the chair last night!' And at the thought he laughed again. Then he went home to dinner.

This evening the scampering of the rats began earlier; indeed it had been going on before his arrival, and only ceased whilst his presence by its freshness disturbed them. After dinner he sat by the fire for a while and had a smoke; and then, having cleared his table, began to work as before. Tonight the rats disturbed him more than they had done on the previous night. How they scampered up and down and under and over! How they squeaked, and scratched, and gnawed! How they, getting bolder by degrees, came to the mouths of their holes and to the chinks and cracks and crannies in the wainscoting till their eyes shone like tiny lamps as the firelight rose and fell. But to him, now doubtless accustomed to them, their eyes were not wicked; only their playfulness touched him. Sometimes the boldest of them made sallies out on the floor or along the mouldings of the wainscot. Now and again as they disturbed him Malcolmson made a sound to frighten them, smiting the table with his hand or giving a fierce 'Hsh, hsh,' so that they fled straightway to their holes.

And so the early part of the night wore on; and despite the noise Malcolmson got more and more immersed in his work.

All at once he stopped, as on the previous night, being overcome by a sudden sense of silence. There was not the faintest sound of gnaw, or scratch, or squeak. The silence was as of the grave. He remembered the odd occurrence of the previous night, and instinctively he looked at the chair standing close by the fireside. And then a very odd sensation thrilled through him.

There, on the great old high-backed carved oak chair beside the fireplace sat the same enormous rat, steadily glaring at him with baleful eyes.

Instinctively he took the nearest thing to his hand, a book of logarithms, and flung it at it. The book was badly aimed and the rat did not stir, so again the poker performance of the previous night was repeated; and again the rat, being closely pursued, fled up the rope of the alarm bell. Strangely too, the departure of this rat was instantly followed by the renewal of the noise made by the general rat community. On this occasion, as on the previous one, Malcolmson could not see at what part of the room the rat disappeared, for the green shade of his lamp left the upper part of the room in darkness, and the fire had burned low.

On looking at his watch he found it was close on midnight; and, not sorry for the *divertissement*, he made up his fire and made himself his nightly pot of tea. He had got through a good spell of work, and thought himself entitled to a cigarette; and so he sat on the great carved oak chair before the fire and enjoyed it. Whilst smoking he began to think that he would like to know where the rat disappeared to, for he had certain ideas for the morrow not entirely disconnected with a rat-trap. Accordingly he lit another lamp and placed it so that it would shine well into the right-hand corner of the wall by the fireplace. Then he got all the books he had with him, and placed them handy to throw at the vermin. Finally he lifted the rope of the alarm bell and placed the end of it on the table, fixing the extreme end under the lamp. As he handled it he could not help noticing how pliable it was, especially for so strong a rope, and one not in use. 'You could hang a man with it,' he thought to himself. When his preparations were made he looked around, and said complacently: 'There now, my friend, I think we shall learn something of you this time!' He began his work again, and though as before somewhat disturbed at first by the noise of the rats, soon lost himself in his propositions and problems.

Again he was called to his immediate surroundings suddenly. This time it might not have been the sudden silence only which took his attention; there was a slight movement of the rope, and the lamp moved. Without stirring, he looked to see if his pile of books was within range, and then cast his eye along the rope. As he looked he saw the great rat drop from the rope on the oak armchair and sit there glaring at him. He raised a book in his right hand, and taking careful aim, flung it at the rat. The latter, with a quick movement, sprang aside and dodged the missile. He then took another book, and a third, and flung them one after another at the rat, but each time unsuccessfully. At last, as he stood with a book poised in his hand to throw, the rat squeaked and seemed afraid. This made Malcolmson more than ever eager to strike, and the book flew and struck the rat a resounding blow. It gave a terrified squeak, and turning on its pursuer a look of terrible malevolence, ran up the chairback and made a great jump to the rope of the alarm bell and ran up it like lightning. The lamp rocked under the sudden strain, but it was a heavy one and did not topple over. Malcolmson kept his eyes on the rat, and saw it by the light of the second lamp leap to a moulding of the wainscot and disappear through a hole in one of the great pictures which hung on the wall, obscured and invisible through its coating of dirt and dust.

'I shall look up my friend's habitation in the morning,' said the student, as he went over to collect his books. 'The third picture from the fireplace; I shall not forget.' He picked up the books one by one, commenting on them as he lifted them. '*Conic Sections* he does not mind, nor *Cycloidal Oscillations*, nor the *Principia*, nor *Quaternions*, nor *Thermodynamics*. Now for the book that fetched him!' Malcolmson took it up and looked at it. As he did so he started, and a sudden pallor overspread his face. He looked round uneasily and shivered slightly, as he murmured to himself:

'The Bible my mother gave me! What an odd coincidence.' He sat down to work again, and the rats in the wainscot renewed their gambols. They did not disturb him, however; somehow their presence gave him a sense of companionship. But he could not attend to his work, and after striving to master the subject on which he was engaged gave it up in despair, and went to bed as the first streak of dawn stole in through the eastern window.

He slept heavily but uneasily, and dreamed much; and when Mrs Dempster woke him late in the morning he seemed ill at ease, and for a few minutes did not seem to realise exactly where he was. His first request rather surprised the servant.

'Mrs Dempster, when I am out today I wish you would get the steps and dust or wash those pictures—specially that one the third from the fireplace—I want to see what they are.'

Late in the afternoon Malcolmson worked at his books in the shaded walk, and the cheerfulness of the previous day came back to him as the day wore on, and he found that his reading was progressing well. He had worked out to a satisfactory conclusion all the problems which had as yet baffled him, and it was in a state of jubilation that he paid a visit to Mrs Witham at 'The Good Traveller'. He found a stranger in the cosy sitting-room with the landlady, who was introduced to him as Dr Thornhill. She was not quite at ease, and this, combined with the Doctor's plunging at once into a series of questions, made Malcolmson come to the conclusion that his presence was not an accident, so without preliminary he said:

'Dr Thornhill, I shall with pleasure answer you any question you may choose to ask me if you will answer me one question first.'

The Doctor seemed surprised, but he smiled and answered at once. 'Done! What is it?'

'Did Mrs Witham ask you to come here and see me and advise me?'

Dr Thornhill for a moment was taken aback, and Mrs Witham got fiery red and turned away; but the Doctor was a frank and ready man, and he answered at once and openly:

'She did: but she didn't intend you to know it. I suppose it was my clumsy haste that made you suspect. She told me that she did not like the idea of your being in that house all by yourself, and that she thought you took too much strong tea. In fact, she wants me to advise you if possible to give up the tea and the very late hours. I was a keen student in my time, so I suppose I may take the liberty of a college man, and without offence, advise you not quite as a stranger.'

Malcolmson with a bright smile held out his hand. 'Shake! as they say in America,' he said. 'I must thank you for your kindness and Mrs Witham too, and your kindness deserves a return on my part. I promise to take no more strong tea—no tea at all till you let me—and I shall go to bed tonight at one o'clock at latest. Will that do?'

'Capital,' said the Doctor. 'Now tell us all that you noticed in the old house,' and so Malcolmson then and there told in minute detail all that had happened in the last two nights. He was interrupted every now and then by some exclamation from Mrs Witham, till finally when he told of the episode of the Bible the landlady's pent-up emotions found vent in a shriek; and it was not till a stiff glass of brandy and water had been administered that she grew composed again. Dr Thornhill listened with a face of growing gravity, and when the narrative was complete and Mrs Witham had been restored he asked:

'The rat always went up the rope of the alarm bell?'

'Always.'

'I suppose you know,' said the Doctor after a pause, 'what the rope is?'

'No!'

'It is,' said the Doctor slowly, 'the very rope which the hangman used for all the victims of the Judge's judicial rancour!' Here he was interrupted by another scream from Mrs Witham, and steps had to be taken for her recovery. Malcolmson having looked at his watch, and found that it was close to his dinner hour, had gone home before her complete recovery.

When Mrs Witham was herself again she almost assailed the Doctor with angry questions as to what he meant by putting such horrible ideas into the poor young man's mind. 'He has quite enough there already to upset him,' she added. Dr Thornhill replied:

'My dear madam, I had a distinct purpose in it! I wanted to draw his attention to the bell rope, and to fix it there. It may be that he is in a highly overwrought state, and has been studying too much, although I am bound to say that he seems as sound and healthy a young man, mentally and bodily, as ever I saw—but then the rats—and that suggestion of the devil.' The doctor shook his head and went on. 'I would have offered to go and stay the first night with him but that I felt sure it would have been a cause of offence. He may get in the night some strange fright or hallucination; and if he does I want him to pull that rope. All alone as he is it will give us warning, and we may reach him in time to be of service. I shall be sitting up pretty late tonight and shall keep my ears open. Do not be alarmed if Benchurch gets a surprise before morning.'

'Oh, Doctor, what do you mean? What do you mean?'

'I mean this; that possibly—nay, more probably—we shall hear the great alarm bell from the Judge's House tonight,' and the Doctor made about as effective an exit as could be thought of.

When Malcolmson arrived home he found that it was a little after his usual time, and Mrs Dempster had gone away—the rules of Greenhow's Charity were not to be neglected. He was glad to see that the place was bright and tidy with a cheerful fire and a well-trimmed lamp. The evening was colder than might have been expected in April, and a heavy wind was blowing with such rapidly-increasing strength that there was every promise of a storm during the night. For a few minutes after his entrance the noise of the rats ceased; but so soon as they became accustomed to his presence they began again. He was glad to hear them, for he felt once more the feeling of companionship in their noise, and his mind ran back to the strange fact that they only ceased to manifest themselves when that other—the great rat with the baleful eyes—came upon the scene. The reading-lamp only was lit and its green shade kept the ceiling and the upper part of the room in darkness, so that the cheerful light from the hearth spreading over the floor and shining on the white cloth laid over the end of the table was warm and cheery. Malcolmson sat down to his dinner with a good appetite and a buoyant spirit. After his dinner and a cigarette he sat steadily down to work, determined not to let anything disturb him, for he remembered his promise to the doctor, and made up his mind to make the best of the time at his disposal.

For an hour or so he worked all right, and then his thoughts began to wander from his books. The actual circumstances around him, the calls on his physical attention, and his nervous susceptibility were not to be denied. By this time the wind had become a gale, and the gale a storm. The old house, solid though it was, seemed to shake to its foundations, and the storm roared and raged through its many chimneys and its queer old gables, producing strange, unearthly sounds in the empty rooms and corridors. Even the great alarm bell on the roof must have felt the force of the wind, for the rope rose and fell slightly, as though the bell were moved a little from time to time, and the limber rope fell on the oak floor with a hard and hollow sound.

As Malcolmson listened to it he bethought himself of the doctor's words, 'It is the rope which the hangman used for the victims of the Judge's judicial rancour,' and he went over to the corner of the fireplace and took it in his hand to look at it. There seemed a sort of deadly interest in it, and as he stood there he lost himself for a moment in speculation as to who these victims were, and the grim wish of the Judge to have such a ghastly relic ever under his eyes. As he stood there the swaying of the bell on the roof still lifted the rope now and again; but presently there came a new sensation—a sort of tremor in the rope, as though something was moving along it.

Looking up instinctively Malcolmson saw the great rat coming slowly down towards him, glaring at him steadily. He dropped the rope and started back with a muttered curse, and the rat turning ran up the rope again and disappeared, and at the same instant Malcolmson became conscious that the noise of the rats, which had ceased for a while, began again.

All this set him thinking, and it occurred to him that he had not investigated the lair of the rat or looked at the pictures, as he had intended. He lit the other lamp without the shade, and, holding it up, went and stood opposite the third picture from the fireplace on the right-hand side where he had seen the rat disappear on the previous night.

At the first glance he started back so suddenly that he almost dropped the lamp, and a deadly pallor overspread his face. His knees shook, and heavy drops of sweat came on his forehead, and he trembled like an aspen. But he was young and plucky, and pulled himself together, and after the pause of a few seconds stepped forward again, raised the lamp, and examined the picture which had been dusted and washed, and now stood out clearly.

It was of a judge dressed in his robes of scarlet and ermine. His face was strong and merciless, evil, crafty, and vindictive, with a sensual mouth, hooked nose of ruddy colour, and shaped like the beak of a bird of prey. The rest of the face was of a cadaverous colour. The eyes were of peculiar brilliance and with a terribly malignant expression. As he looked at them, Malcolmson grew cold, for he saw there the very counterpart of the eyes of the great rat. The lamp almost fell from his hand, he saw the rat with its baleful eyes peering out through the hole in the corner of the picture, and noted the sudden cessation of the noise of the other rats. However, he pulled himself together, and went on with his examination of the picture.

The Judge was seated in a great high-backed carved oak chair, on the right-hand side of a great stone fireplace where, in the corner, a rope hung down from the ceiling, its end lying coiled on the floor. With a feeling of something like horror, Malcolmson recognised the scene of the room as it stood, and gazed around him in an awe-struck manner as though he expected to find some strange presence behind him. Then he looked over to the corner of the fireplace—and with a loud cry he let the lamp fall from his hand.

There, in the Judge's armchair, with the rope hanging behind, sat the rat with the Judge's baleful eyes, now intensified and with a fiendish leer. Save for the howling of the storm without there was silence.

The fallen lamp recalled Malcolmson to himself. Fortunately it was of metal, and so the oil was not spilt. However, the practical need of attending to it settled at once his nervous apprehensions. When he had turned it out, he wiped his brow and thought for a moment.

'This will not do,' he said to himself. 'If I go on like this I shall become a crazy fool. This must stop! I promised the Doctor I would not take tea. Faith, he was pretty right! My nerves must have been getting into a queer state. Funny I did not notice it. I never felt better in my life. However, it is all right now, and I shall not be such a fool again.'

Then he mixed himself a good stiff glass of brandy and water and resolutely sat down to his work.

It was nearly an hour when he looked up from his book, disturbed by the sudden stillness. Without, the wind howled and roared louder than ever, and the rain drove in sheets against the windows, beating like hail on the glass; but within there was no sound whatever save the echo of the wind as it roared in the great chimney, and now and then a hiss as a few raindrops found their way down the chimney in a lull of the storm. The fire had fallen low and had ceased to flame, though it threw out a red glow. Malcolmson listened attentively, and presently heard a thin, squeaking noise, very faint. It came from the corner of the room where the rope hung down, and he thought it was the creaking of the rope on the floor as the swaying of the bell raised and lowered it. Looking up, however, he saw in the dim light the great rat clinging to the rope and gnawing it. The rope was already nearly gnawed through—he could see the lighter colour where the strands were laid bare. As he looked the job was completed, and the severed end of the rope fell clattering on the oaken floor, whilst for an instant the great rat remained like a knob or tassel at the end of the rope, which now began to sway to and fro. Malcolmson felt for a moment another pang of terror as he thought that now the possibility of calling the outer world to his assistance was cut off, but an intense anger took its place, and seizing the book he was reading he hurled it at the rat. The blow was well aimed, but before the missile could reach it the rat dropped off and struck the floor with a soft thud. Malcolmson instantly rushed over towards it, but it darted away and disappeared in the darkness of the shadows of the room. Malcolmson felt that his work was over for the night, and determined then and there to vary the monotony of the proceedings by a hunt for the rat, and took off the green shade of the lamp so as to insure a wider spreading light. As he did so the gloom of the upper part of the room was relieved, and in the new flood of light, great by comparison with the previous darkness, the pictures on the wall stood out boldly. From where he stood, Malcolmson saw right opposite to him the third picture on the wall from the right of the fireplace. He rubbed his eyes in surprise, and then a great fear began to come upon him.

In the centre of the picture was a great irregular patch of brown canvas, as fresh as when it was stretched on the frame. The background was as before, with chair and chimney-corner and rope, but the figure of the Judge had disappeared.

Malcolmson, almost in a chill of horror, turned slowly round, and then he began to shake and tremble like a man in a palsy. His strength seemed to have left him, and he was incapable of action or movement, hardly even of thought. He could only see and hear.

There, on the great high-backed carved oak chair sat the Judge in his robes of scarlet and ermine, with his baleful eyes glaring vindictively, and a smile of triumph on the resolute, cruel mouth, as he lifted with his hands a *black cap*. Malcolmson felt as if the blood was running from his heart, as one does in moments of prolonged suspense. There was a singing in his ears. Without, he could hear the roar and howl of the tempest, and through it, swept on the storm, came the striking of midnight by the great chimes in the market place. He stood for a space of time that seemed to him endless, still as a statue and with wide-open, horror-struck eyes, breathless. As the clock struck, so the smile of triumph on the Judge's face intensified, and at the last stroke of midnight he placed the black cap on his head.

Slowly and deliberately the Judge rose from his chair and picked up the piece of rope of the alarm bell which lay on the floor, drew it through his hands as if he enjoyed its touch, and then deliberately began to knot one end of it, fashioning it into a noose. This he tightened and tested with his foot, pulling hard at it till he was satisfied and then making a running noose of it, which he held in his hand. Then he began to move along the table on the opposite side to Malcolmson, keeping his eyes on him until he had passed him, when with a quick movement he stood in front of the door. Malcolmson then began to feel that he was trapped, and tried to think of what he should do. There was some fascination in the Judge's eyes, which he never took off him, and he had, perforce, to look. He saw the Judge approach—still keeping between him and the door—and raise the noose and throw it towards him as if to entangle him. With a great effort he made a quick movement to one side, and saw the rope fall beside him, and heard it strike the oaken floor. Again the Judge raised the noose and tried to ensnare him, ever keeping his baleful eyes fixed on him, and each time by a mighty effort the student just managed to evade it. So this went on for many times, the Judge seeming never discouraged nor discomposed at failure, but playing as a cat does with a mouse. At last in despair, which had reached its climax, Malcolmson cast a quick glance round him. The lamp seemed to have blazed up, and there was a fairly good light in the room. At the many rat-holes and in the chinks and crannies of the wainscot he saw the rats' eyes; and this aspect, that was purely physical, gave him a gleam of comfort. He looked around and saw that the rope of the great alarm bell was laden with rats. Every inch of it was covered with them, and more and more were pouring through the small circular hole in the ceiling whence it emerged, so that with their weight the bell was beginning to sway.

Hark! it had swayed till the clapper had touched the bell. The sound was but a tiny one, but the bell was only beginning to sway, and it would increase.

At the sound the Judge, who had been keeping his eyes fixed on Malcolmson, looked up, and a scowl of diabolical anger overspread his face. His eyes fairly glowed like hot coals, and he stamped his foot with a sound that seemed to make the house shake. A dreadful peal of thunder broke overhead as he raised the rope again, whilst the rats kept running up and down the rope as though working against time. This time, instead of throwing it, he drew close to his victim, and held open the noose as he approached. As he came closer there seemed something paralysing in his very presence, and Malcolmson stood rigid as a corpse. He felt the Judge's icy fingers touch his throat as he adjusted the rope. The noose tightened—tightened. Then the Judge, taking the rigid form of the student in his arms, carried him over and placed him standing in the oak chair, and stepping up beside him, put his hand up and caught the end of the swaying rope of the alarm bell. As he raised his hand the rats fled squeaking, and disappeared through the hole in the ceiling. Taking the end of the noose which was round Malcolmson's neck he tied it to the hanging bell-rope, and then descending pulled away the chair.

When the alarm bell of the Judge's House began to sound a crowd soon assembled. Lights and torches of various kinds appeared, and soon a silent crowd was hurrying to the spot. They knocked loudly at the door, but there was no reply. Then they burst in the door, and poured into the great dining-room, the Doctor at the head.

There at the end of the rope of the great alarm bell hung the body of the student, and on the face of the Judge in the picture was a malignant smile.

A Ghost Story

JEROME K. JEROME

I MET a man in the Strand one day that I knew very well, as I thought, though I had not seen him for years. We walked together to Charing Cross, and there we shook hands and parted. Next morning, I spoke of this meeting to a mutual friend, and then I learnt, for the first time, that the man had died six months before.

The natural inference was that I had mistaken one man for another, an error that, not having a good memory for faces, I frequently fall into. What was remarkable about the matter, however, was that throughout our walk I had conversed with the man under the impression that he was that other dead man, and, whether by coincidence or not, his replies had never once suggested to me my mistake.

As soon as I finished speaking, Jephson, who had been listening very thoughtfully, asked me if I believed in spiritualism 'to its fullest extent'.

'That is rather a large question,' I answered. 'What do you mean by "spiritualism to its fullest extent"?'

'Well, do you believe that the spirits of the dead have not only the power of revisiting this earth at their will, but that, when here, they have the power of action, or rather, of exciting to action. Let me put a definite case. A spiritualist friend of mine, a sensible and by no means imaginative man, once told me that a table, through the medium of which the spirit of a friend had been in the habit of communicating with him, came slowly across the room towards him, of its own accord, one night as he sat alone, and pinioned him against the wall. Now can any of you believe that, or can't you?'

'I could,' Brown took it upon himself to reply; 'but, before doing so, I should wish for an introduction to the friend who told you the story. Speaking generally,' he continued, 'it seems to me that the difference between what we call the natural and the supernatural is merely the difference between frequency and rarity of occurrence. Having regard to the phenomena we are compelled to admit, I think it illogical to disbelieve anything that we are not able to disprove.'

'For my part,' remarked MacShaugnassy, 'I can believe in the ability of our spirit friends to give the quaint entertainments credited to them much easier than I can in their desire to do so.'

'You mean,' added Jephson, 'that you cannot understand why a spirit, not compelled as we are by the exigencies of society, should care to spend

47

its evenings carrying on a laboured and childish conversation with a room full of abnormally uninteresting people.'

'That is precisely what I cannot understand,' MacShaugnassy agreed.

'Nor I, either,' said Jephson. 'But I was thinking of something very different altogether. Suppose a man died with the dearest wish of his heart unfulfilled, do you believe that his spirit might have power to return to earth and complete the interrupted work?'

'Well,' answered MacShaugnassy, 'if one admits the possibility of spirits retaining any interest in the affairs of this world at all, it is certainly more reasonable to imagine·them engaged upon a task such as you suggest, than to believe that they occupy themselves with the performance of mere drawing-room tricks. But what are you leading up to?'

'Why to this,' replied Jephson, seating himself straddle-legged across his chair, and leaning his arms upon the back. 'I was told a story this morning at the hospital by an old French doctor. The actual facts are few and simple; all that is known can be read in the Paris police records of forty-two years ago.

'The most important part of the case, however, is the part that is not known, and that never will be known. ˉ

'The story begins with a great wrong done by one man unto another man. What the wrong was I do not know. I am inclined to think, however, it was connected with a woman. I think that because he who had been wronged hated him who had wronged with a hate such as does not often burn in a man's brain unless it be fanned by the memory of a woman's breath.

'Still that is only conjecture, and the point is immaterial. The man who had done the wrong fled, and the other man followed him. It became a point to·point race, the first man having the advantage of a day's start. The course was the whole world, and the stakes were the first man's life.

'Travellers were few and far between in those days, and this made the trail easy to follow. The first man, never knowing how far or how near the other was behind him, and hoping now and again that he might have baffled him, would rest for a while. The second man, knowing always just how far the first one was before him, never paused, and thus each day the man who was spurred by Hate drew nearer to the man who was spurred by Fear.

'At this town the answer to the never-varied question would be:

·' "At seven o'clock last evening, M'sieur."

·' "Seven—ah; eighteen hours. Give me something to eat, quick, while the horses are being put to."

'At the next the calculation would be sixteen hours.

'Passing a lonely châlet, Monsieur puts his head out of the window:

' "How long since a carriage passed this way, with a tall, fair man inside?"

' "Such a one passed early this morning, M'sieur."

' "Thanks, drive on, a hundred francs apiece if you are through the pass before daybreak."

' "And what for dead horses, M'sieur?"

' "Twice their value when living."

'One day the man who was ridden by Fear looked up, and saw before him the open door of a cathedral, and, passing in, knelt down and prayed. He prayed long and fervently, for men, when they are in sore straits, clutch eagerly at the straws of faith. He prayed that he might be forgiven his sin, and, more important still, that he might be pardoned the consequences of his sin, and be delivered from his adversary; and a few chairs from him, facing him, knelt his enemy, praying also.

'But the second man's prayer, being a thanksgiving merely, was short, so that when the first man raised his eyes, he saw the face of his enemy gazing at him across the chair tops, with a mocking smile upon it.

'He made no attempt to rise, but remained kneeling, fascinated by the look of joy that shone out of the other man's eyes. And the other man moved the high-backed chairs one by one, and came towards him softly.

'Then, just as the man who had been wronged stood beside the man who had wronged him, full of gladness that his opportunity had come, there burst from the cathedral tower a sudden clash of bells, and the man whose opportunity had come broke his heart and fell back dead, with that mocking smile of his still playing round his mouth.

'And so he lay there.

'Then the man who had done the wrong rose up and passed out, praising God.

'What became of the body of the other man is not known. It was the body of a stranger who had died suddenly in the cathedral. There was none to identify it, none to claim it.

'Years passed away, and the survivor in the tragedy became a worthy and useful citizen, and a noted man of science.

'In his laboratory were many objects necessary to him in his researches, and prominent among them, stood in a certain corner, a human skeleton. It was a very old and much-mended skeleton, and one day the long-expected end arrived, and it tumbled to pieces.

'Thus it became necessary to purchase another.

'The man of science visited a dealer he well knew; a little parchment-faced old man who kept a dingy shop, where nothing was ever sold, within the shadow of the towers of Notre Dame.

'The little parchment-faced old man had just the very thing that Monsieur wanted—a singularly fine and well-proportioned "study". It should be sent round and set up in Monsieur's laboratory that very afternoon.

'The dealer was as good as his word. When Monsieur entered his laboratory that evening, the thing was in its place.

'Monsieur seated himself in his high-backed chair, and tried to collect his thoughts. But Monsieur's thoughts were unruly, and inclined to wander, and to wander always in one direction.

'Monsieur opened a large volume and commenced to read. He read of a man who had wronged another and fled from him, the other man following. Finding himself reading this, he closed the book angrily, and went and stood by the window and looked out. He saw before him the sun-pierced nave of a great cathedral, and on the stones lay a dead man with a mocking smile upon his face.

'Cursing himself for a fool, he turned away with a laugh. But his laugh was short-lived, for it seemed to him that something else in the room was laughing also. Struck suddenly still, with his feet glued to the ground, he stood listening for awhile: then sought with starting eyes the corner from where the sound had seemed to come. But the white thing standing there was only grinning.

'Monsieur wiped the damp sweat from his head and hands, and stole out.

'For a couple of days he did not enter the room again. On the third, telling himself that his fears were those of a hysterical girl, he opened the door and went in. To shame himself, he took his lamp in his hand, and crossing over to the far corner where the skeleton stood, examined it. A set of bones bought for a hundred francs. Was he a child, to be scared by such a bogey!

'He held his lamp up in front of the thing's grinning head. The flame of the lamp flickered as though a faint breath had passed over it.

'The man explained this to himself by saying that the walls of the house were old and cracked, and that the wind might creep in anywhere. He repeated this explanation to himself as he recrossed the room, walking backwards, with his eyes fixed on the thing. When he reached his desk, he sat down and gripped the arms of his chair till his fingers turned white.

'He tried to work, but the empty sockets in that grinning head seemed to be drawing him towards them. He rose and battled with his inclination to fly screaming from the room. Glancing fearfully about him, his eye fell upon a high screen, standing before the door. He dragged it forward, and placed it between himself and the thing, so that he could not see it—

nor it see him. Then he sat down again to his work. For awhile he forced himself to look at the book in front of him, but at last, unable to control himself any longer, he suffered his eyes to follow their own bent.

'It may have been an hallucination. He may have accidentally placed the screen so as to favour such an illusion. But what he saw was a bony hand coming round the corner of the screen, and, with a cry, he fell to the floor in a swoon.

'The people of the house came running in, and lifting him up, carried him out, and laid him upon his bed. As soon as he recovered, his first question was, where had they found the thing—where was it when they entered the room? and when they told him they had seen it standing where it always stood, and had gone down into the room to look again, because of his frenzied entreaties, and returned trying to hide their smiles, he listened to their talk about overwork, and the necessity for change and rest, and said they might do with him as they would.

'So for many months the laboratory door remained locked. Then there came a chill autumn evening when the man of science opened it again, and closed it behind him.

'He lighted his lamp, and gathered his instruments and books around him, and sat down before them in his high-backed chair. And the old terror returned to him.

'But this time he meant to conquer himself. His nerves were stronger now, and his brain clearer; he would fight his unreasoning fear. He crossed to the door and locked himself in, and flung the key to the other end of the room, where it fell among jars and bottles with an echoing clatter.

'Later on, his old housekeeper, going her final round, tapped at his door and wished him good night, as was her custom. She received no response, at first, and, growing nervous, tapped louder and called again; and at length an answering "good night" came back to her.

'She thought little about it at the time, but afterwards she remembered that the voice that had replied to her had been strangely grating and mechanical. Trying to describe it, she likened it to such a voice as she would imagine coming from a statue.

'Next morning his door remained still locked. It was no unusual thing for him to work all night, and far into the next day, so no one thought to be surprised. When, however, evening came, and yet he did not appear, his servants gathered outside the room and whispered, remembering what had happened once before.

'They listened, but could hear no sound. They shook the door and called to him, then beat with their fists upon the wooden panels. But still no sound came from the room.

'Becoming alarmed, they decided to burst open the door, and, after many blows, it gave way and flew back, and they crowded in.

'He sat bolt upright in his high-backed chair. They thought at first he had died in his sleep. But when they drew nearer and the light fell upon him, they saw the livid marks of bony fingers round his throat; and in his eyes there was a terror such as is not often seen in human eyes.'

Brown was the first to break the silence that followed. He asked me if I had any brandy on board. He said he felt he should like just a nip of brandy before going to bed. That is one of the chief charms of Jephson's stories: they always make you feel you want a little brandy.

The Moonlit Road

AMBROSE BIERCE

I

STATEMENT OF JOEL HETMAN, JR.

I AM the most unfortunate of men. Rich, respected, fairly well educated and of sound health—with many other advantages usually valued by those having them and coveted by those who have them not—I sometimes think that I should be less unhappy if they had been denied me, for then the contrast between my outer and my inner life would not be continually demanding a painful attention. In the stress of privation and the need of effort I might sometimes forget the somber secret ever baffling the conjecture that it compels.

I am the only child of Joel and Julia Hetman. The one was a well-to-do country gentleman, the other a beautiful and accomplished woman to whom he was passionately attached with what I now know to have been a jealous and exacting devotion. The family home was a few miles from Nashville, Tennessee, a large, irregularly built dwelling of no particular order of architecture, a little way off the road, in a park of trees and shrubbery.

At the time of which I write I was nineteen years old, a student at Yale. One day I received a telegram from my father of such urgency that in compliance with its unexplained demand I left at once for home. At the railway station in Nashville a distant relative awaited me to apprise me of the reason for my recall: my mother had been barbarously murdered— why and by whom none could conjecture, but the circumstances were these:

My father had gone to Nashville, intending to return the next afternoon. Something prevented his accomplishing the business in hand, so he returned on the same night, arriving just before the dawn. In his testimony before the coroner he explained that having no latchkey and not caring to disturb the sleeping servants, he had, with no clearly defined intention, gone round to the rear of the house. As he turned an angle of the building, he heard a sound as of a door gently closed, and saw in the darkness, indistinctly, the figure of a man, which instantly disappeared among the trees of the lawn. A hasty pursuit and brief search of the grounds in the belief that the trespasser was some one secretly visiting a servant proving fruitless, he entered at the unlocked door and mounted the stairs to my mother's chamber. Its door was open, and stepping into black darkness he fell headlong over some heavy object on the floor. I may spare myself the details; it was my poor mother, dead of strangulation by human hands!

Nothing had been taken from the house, the servants had heard no sound, and excepting those terrible finger-marks upon the dead woman's throat—dear God! that I might forget them!—no trace of the assassin was ever found.

I gave up my studies and remained with my father, who, naturally, was greatly changed. Always of a sedate, taciturn disposition, he now fell into so deep a dejection that nothing could hold his attention, yet anything—a foot-fall, the sudden closing of a door—aroused in him a fitful interest; one might have called it an apprehension. At any small surprise of the senses he would start visibly and sometimes turn pale, then relapse into a melancholy apathy deeper than before. I suppose he was what is called a "nervous wreck." As to me, I was younger then than now—there is much in that. Youth is Gilead, in which is balm for every wound. Ah, that I might again dwell in that enchanted land! Unacquainted with grief, I knew not how to appraise my bereavement; I could not rightly estimate the strength of the stroke.

One night, a few months after the dreadful event, my father and I walked home from the city. The full moon was about three hours above the eastern horizon; the entire countryside had the solemn stillness of a summer night; our footfalls and the ceaseless song of the katydids were the only sound aloof. Black shadows of bordering trees lay athwart the road, which, in the short reaches between, gleamed a ghostly white. As we approached the gate to our dwelling, whose front was in shadow, and in which no light shone, my father suddenly stopped and clutched my arm, saying, hardly above his breath:

"God! God! what is that?"

"I hear nothing," I replied.

"But see—see!" he said, pointing along the road, directly ahead.

I said: "Nothing is there. Come, father, let us go in—you are ill."

He had released my arm and was standing rigid and motionless in the center of the illuminated roadway, staring like one bereft of sense. His face in the moonlight showed a pallor and fixity inexpressibly distressing. I pulled gently at his sleeve, but he had forgotten my existence. Presently he began to retire backward, step by step, never for an instant removing his eyes from what he saw, or thought he saw. I turned half round to follow, but stood irresolute. I do not recall any feeling of fear, unless a sudden chill was its physical manifestation. It seemed as if an icy wind had touched my face and enfolded my body from head to foot; I could feel the stir of it in my hair.

At that moment my attention was drawn to a light that suddenly streamed from an upper window of the house: one of the servants, awakened by what mysterious premonition of evil who can say, and in obedience to an impulse that she was never able to name, had lit a lamp. When I turned to look for my father he was gone, and in all the years that have passed no whisper of his fate has come across the borderland of conjecture from the realm of the unknown.

II

STATEMENT OF CASPAR GRATTAN

To-day I am said to live; to-morrow, here in this room, will lie a senseless shape of clay that all too long was I. If anyone lift the cloth from the face of that unpleasant thing it will be in gratification of a mere morbid curiosity. Some, doubtless, will go further and inquire, "Who was he?" In this writing I supply the only answer that I am able to make—Caspar Grattan. Surely, that should be enough. The name has served my small need for more than twenty years of a life of unknown length. True, I gave it to myself, but lacking another I had the right. In this world one must have a name; it prevents confusion, even when it does not establish identity. Some, though, are known by numbers, which also seem inadequate distinctions.

One day, for illustration, I was passing along a street of a city, far from here, when I met two men in uniform, one of whom, half pausing and looking curiously into my face, said to his companion, "That man looks like 767." Something in the number seemed familiar and horrible. Moved by an uncontrollable impulse, I sprang into a side street and ran until I fell exhausted in a country lane.

I have never forgotten that number, and always it comes to memory attended by gibbering obscenity, peals of joyless laughter, the clang of iron doors. So I say a name, even if self-bestowed, is better than a number. In the register of the potter's field I shall soon have both. What wealth!

Of him who shall find this paper I must beg a little consideration. It is not the history of my life; the knowledge to write that is denied me. This is only a record of broken and apparently unrelated memories, some of them as distinct and sequent as brilliant beads upon a thread, others remote and strange, having the character of crimson dreams with interspaces blank and black—witch-fires glowing still and red in a great desolation.

Standing upon the shore of eternity, I turn for a last look landward over the course by which I came. There are twenty years of footprints fairly distinct, the impressions of bleeding feet. They lead through poverty and pain, devious and unsure, as of one staggering beneath a burden—

Remote, unfriended, melancholy, slow.

Ah, the poet's prophecy of Me—how admirable, how dreadfully admirable!

Backward beyond the beginning of this *via dolorosa*—this epic of suffering with episodes of sin—I see nothing clearly; it comes out of a cloud. I know that it spans only twenty years, yet I am an old man.

One does not remember one's birth—one has to be told. But with me it was different; life came to me full-handed and dowered me with all my faculties and powers. Of a previous existence I know no more than others, for all have stammering intimations that may be memories and may be dreams. I know only that my first consciousness was of maturity in body and mind—a consciousness accepted without surprise or conjecture. I merely found myself walking in a forest, half-clad, footsore, unutterably weary and hungry. Seeing a farmhouse, I approached and asked for food, which was given me by one who inquired my name. I did not know, yet knew that all had names. Greatly embarrassed, I retreated, and night coming on, lay down in the forest and slept.

The next day I entered a large town which I shall not name. Nor shall I recount further incidents of the life that is now to end—a life of wandering, always and everywhere haunted by an overmastering sense of crime in punishment of wrong and of terror in punishment of crime. Let me see if I can reduce it to narrative.

I seem once to have lived near a great city, a prosperous planter, married to a woman whom I loved and distrusted. We had, it sometimes seems, one child, a youth of brilliant parts and promise. He is at all times a vague figure, never clearly drawn, frequently altogether out of the picture.

One luckless evening it occurred to me to test my wife's fidelity in a vulgar, commonplace way familiar to everyone who has acquaintance with the literature of fact and fiction. I went to the city, telling my wife that I should be absent until the following afternoon. But I returned before daybreak and went to the rear of the house, purposing to enter by a door with which I had secretly so tampered that it would seem to lock, yet not actually fasten. As I approached it, I heard it gently open and close, and saw a man steal away into the darkness. With murder in my heart, I sprang after him, but he had vanished without even the bad luck of identification. Sometimes now I cannot even persuade myself that it was a human being.

Crazed with jealousy and rage, blind and bestial with all the elemental passions of insulted manhood, I entered the house and sprang up the stairs to the door of my wife's chamber. It was closed, but having tampered with its lock also, I easily entered and despite the black darkness soon stood by the side of her bed. My groping hands told me that although disarranged it was unoccupied.

"She is below," I thought, "and terrified by my entrance has evaded me in the darkness of the hall."

With the purpose of seeking her I turned to leave the room, but took a wrong direction—the right one! My foot struck her, cowering in a corner of the room. Instantly my hands were at her throat, stifling a shriek, my knees were upon her struggling body; and there in the darkness, without a word of accusation or reproach, I strangled her till she died!

There ends the dream. I have related it in the past tense, but the present would be the fitter form, for again and again the somber tragedy reenacts itself in my consciousness—over and over I lay the plan, I suffer the confirmation, I redress the wrong. Then all is blank; and afterward the rains beat against the grimy window-panes, or the snows fall upon my scant attire, the wheels rattle in the squalid streets where my life lies in poverty and mean employment. If there is ever sunshine I do not recall it; if there are birds they do not sing.

There is another dream, another vision of the night. I stand among the shadows in a moonlit road. I am aware of another presence, but whose I cannot rightly determine. In the shadow of a great dwelling I catch the gleam of white garments; then the figure of a woman confronts me in the road—my murdered wife! There is death in the face; there are marks upon the throat. The eyes are fixed on mine with an infinite gravity which is not reproach, nor hate, nor menace, nor anything less terrible than recognition. Before this awful apparition I retreat in terror—a terror that is upon me as I write. I can no longer rightly shape the words. See! they—

Now I am calm, but truly there is no more to tell: the incident ends where it began—in darkness and in doubt.

Yes, I am again in control of myself: "the captain of my soul." But that is not respite; it is another stage and phase of expiation. My penance, constant in degree, is mutable in kind: one of its variants is tranquillity. After all, it is only a life-sentence. "To Hell for life"—that is a foolish penalty: the culprit chooses the duration of his punishment. To-day my term expires.

To each and all, the peace that was not mine.

III

STATEMENT OF THE LATE JULIA HETMAN, THROUGH THE MEDIUM BAYROLLES

I had retired early and fallen almost immediately into a peaceful sleep, from which I awoke with that indefinable sense of peril which is, I think, a common experience in that other, earlier life. Of its unmeaning character, too, I was entirely persuaded, yet that did not banish it. My husband, Joel Hetman, was away from home; the servants slept in another part of the house. But these were familiar conditions; they had never before distressed me. Nevertheless, the strange terror grew so insupportable that conquering my reluctance to move I sat up and lit the lamp at my bedside. Contrary to my expectation this gave me no relief; the light seemed rather an added danger, for I reflected that it would shine out under the door, disclosing my presence to whatever evil thing might lurk outside. You that are still in the flesh, subject to horrors of the imagination, think what a monstrous fear that must be which seeks in darkness security from malevolent existences of the night. That is to spring to close quarters with an unseen enemy—the strategy of despair!

Extinguishing the lamp I pulled the bed-clothing about my head and lay trembling and silent, unable to shriek, forgetful to pray. In this pitiable state I must have lain for what you call hours—with us there are no hours, there is no time.

At last it came—a soft, irregular sound of footfalls on the stairs! They were slow, hesitant, uncertain, as of something that did not see its way; to my disordered reason all the more terrifying for that, as the approach of some blind and mindless malevolence to which is no appeal. I even thought that I must have left the hall lamp burning and the groping of this creature proved it a monster of the night. This was foolish and inconsistent with my previous dread of the light, but what would you have? Fear has no brains; it is an idiot. The dismal witness that it bears and the cowardly counsel that it whispers are unrelated. We know this well, we who have passed into the Realm of Terror, who skulk in eternal dusk among the scenes of our former lives, invisible even to ourselves and one another, yet hiding forlorn in lonely places; yearning for speech with our loved ones, yet dumb, and as fearful of them as they of us. Sometimes the disability is removed, the law suspended: by the deathless power of love or hate we break the spell—we are seen by those whom we would warn, console, or punish. What form we seem to them to bear we know not; we know only that we terrify even those whom we most wish to comfort, and from whom we most crave tenderness and sympathy.

Forgive, I pray you, this inconsequent digression by what was once a woman. You who consult us in this imperfect way—you do not understand. You ask foolish questions about things unknown and things forbidden. Much that we know and could impart in our speech is meaningless in yours. We must communicate with you through a stammering intelligence in that small fraction of our language that you yourselves can speak. You think that we are of another world. No, we have knowledge of no world but yours, though for us it holds no sunlight, no warmth, no music, no laughter, no song of birds, nor any companionship. O God! what a thing it is to be a ghost, cowering and shivering in an altered world, a prey to apprehension and despair!

No, I did not die of fright: the Thing turned and went away. I heard it go down the stairs, hurriedly, I thought, as if itself in sudden fear. Then I rose to call for help. Hardly had my shaking hand found the doorknob when—merciful heaven!—I heard it returning. Its footfalls as it remounted the stairs were rapid, heavy and loud; they shook the house. I fled to an angle of the wall and crouched upon the floor. I tried to pray. I tried to call the name of my dear husband. Then I heard the door thrown open. There was an interval of unconsciousness, and when I revived I felt a strangling clutch upon my throat—felt my arms feebly beating against something that bore me backward—felt my tongue thrusting itself from between my teeth! And then I passed into this life.

No, I have no knowledge of what it was. The sum of what we knew at death is the measure of what we know afterward of all that went before. Of this existence we know many things, but no new light falls upon any page of that; in memory is written all of it that we can read. Here are no heights of truth overlooking the confused landscape of that dubitable domain. We still dwell in the Valley of the Shadow, lurk in its desolate places, peering from brambles and thickets at its mad, malign inhabitants. How should we have new knowledge of that fading past?

What I am about to relate happened on a night. We know when it is night, for then you retire to your houses and we can venture from our places of concealment to move unafraid about our old homes, to look in at the windows, even to enter and gaze upon your faces as you sleep. I had lingered long near the dwelling where I had been so cruelly changed to what I am, as we do while any that we love or hate remain. Vainly I had sought some method of manifestation, some way to make my continued existence and my great love and poignant pity understood by my husband and son. Always if they slept they would wake, or if in my desperation I dared approach them when they were awake, would turn toward me the terrible eyes of the living, frightening me by the glances that I sought from the purpose that I held.

On this night I had searched for them without success, fearing to find them; they were nowhere in the house, nor about the moonlit lawn. For, although the sun is lost to us forever, the moon, full-orbed or slender, remains to us. Sometimes it shines by night, sometimes by day, but always it rises and sets, as in that other life.

I left the lawn and moved in the white light and silence along the road, aimless and sorrowing. Suddenly I heard the voice of my poor husband in exclamations of astonishment, with that of my son in reassurance and dissuasion; and there by the shadow of a group of trees they stood—near, so near! Their faces were toward me, the eyes of the elder man fixed upon mine. He saw me—at last, at last, he saw me! In the consciousness of that, my terror fled as a cruel dream. The death-spell was broken: Love had conquered Law! Mad with exultation I shouted—I *must* have shouted, "He sees, he sees: he will understand!" Then, controlling myself, I moved forward, smiling and consciously beautiful, to offer myself to his arms, to comfort him with endearments, and, with my son's hand in mine, to speak words that should restore the broken bonds between the living and the dead.

Alas! alas! his face went white with fear, his eyes were as those of a hunted animal. He backed away from me, as I advanced, and at last turned and fled into the wood—whither, it is not given to me to know.

To my poor boy, left doubly desolate, I have never been able to impart a sense of my presence. Soon he, too, must pass to this Life Invisible and be lost to me forever.

The Monkey's Paw

W. W. JACOBS

I

WITHOUT, THE NIGHT was cold and wet, but in the small parlour of Laburnum Villa the blinds were drawn and the fire burned brightly. Father and son were at chess; the former, who possessed ideas about the game involving radical changes, putting his king into such sharp and unnecessary perils that it even provoked comment from the white-haired old lady knitting placidly by the fire.

'Hark at the wind,' said Mr White, who, having seen a fatal mistake after it was too late, was amiably desirous of preventing his son from seeing it.

'I'm listening,' said the latter, grimly surveying the board as he stretched out his hand. 'Check.'

'I should hardly think that he'd come tonight,' said his father, with his hand poised over the board.

'Mate,' replied the son.

'That's the worst of living so far out,' bawled Mr White, with sudden and unlooked-for violence; 'of all the beastly, slushy, out-of-the-way places to live in, this is the worst. Path's a bog, and the road's a torrent. I don't know what people are thinking about. I suppose because only two houses in the road are let, they think it doesn't matter.'

'Never mind, dear,' said his wife soothingly; 'perhaps you'll win the next one.'

Mr White looked up sharply, just in time to intercept a knowing glance between mother and son. The words died away on his lips, and he hid a guilty grin in his thin grey beard.

'There he is,' said Herbert White, as the gate banged to loudly and heavy footsteps came toward the door.

The old man rose with hospitable haste, and opening the door, was heard condoling with the new arrival. The new arrival also condoled with himself, so that Mrs White said, 'Tut, tut!' and coughed gently as her husband entered the room, followed by a tall, burly man, beady of eye and rubicund of visage.

'Sergeant-Major Morris,' he said, introducing him.

The sergeant-major shook hands, and taking the proffered seat by the fire, watched contentedly while his host got out whisky and tumblers and stood a small copper kettle on the fire.

At the third glass his eyes got brighter, and he began to talk, the little family circle regarding with eager interest this visitor from distant parts, as he squared his broad shoulders in the chair and spoke of wild scenes and doughty deeds; of wars and plagues and strange peoples.

'Twenty-one years of it,' said Mr White, nodding at his wife and son. 'When he went away he was a slip of a youth in the warehouse. Now look at him.'

'He don't look to have taken much harm,' said Mrs White politely.

'I'd like to go to India myself,' said the old man, 'just to look round a bit, you know.'

'Better where you are,' said the sergeant-major, shaking his head. He put down the empty glass, and sighing softly, shook it again.

'I should like to see those old temples and fakirs and jugglers,' said the old man. 'What was that you started telling me the other day about a monkey's paw or something, Morris?'

'Nothing,' said the soldier hastily. 'Leastways nothing worth hearing.'

'Monkey's paw?' said Mrs White curiously.

'Well, it's just a bit of what you might call magic, perhaps,' said the sergeant-major offhandedly.

His three listeners leaned forward eagerly. The visitor absentmindedly put his empty glass to his lips and then set it down again. His host filled it for him.

'To look at,' said the sergeant-major, fumbling in his pocket, 'it's just an ordinary little paw, dried to a mummy.'

He took something out of his pocket and proffered it. Mrs White drew back with a grimace, but her son, taking it, examined it curiously.

'And what is there special about it?' inquired Mr White as he took it from his son, and having examined it, placed it upon the table.

'It had a spell put on it by an old fakir,' said the sergeant-major, 'a very holy man. He wanted to show that fate ruled people's lives, and that those who interfered with it did so to their sorrow. He put a spell on it so that three separate men could each have three wishes from it.'

His manner was so impressive that his hearers were conscious that their light laughter jarred somewhat.

'Well, why don't you have three, sir?' said Herbert White cleverly.

The soldier regarded him in the way that middle age is wont to regard presumptuous youth. 'I have,' he said quietly, and his blotchy face whitened.

'And did you really have the three wishes granted?' asked Mrs White.

'I did,' said the sergeant-major, and his glass tapped against his strong teeth.

'And has anybody else wished?' persisted the old lady.

'The first man had his three wishes. Yes,' was the reply; 'I don't know what the first two were, but the third was for death. That's how I got the paw.'

His tones were so grave that a hush fell upon the group.

'If you've had your three wishes, it's no good to you now, then, Morris,' said the old man at last. 'What do you keep it for?'

The soldier shook his head. 'Fancy, I suppose,' he said slowly. 'I did have some idea of selling it, but I don't think I will. It has caused enough mischief already. Besides, people won't buy. They think it's a fairy tale, some of them; and those who do think anything of it want to try it first and pay me afterward.'

'If you could have another three wishes,' said the old man, eyeing him keenly, 'would you have them?'

'I don't know,' said the other. 'I don't know.'

He took the paw, and dangling it between his forefinger and thumb, suddenly threw it upon the fire. White, with a slight cry, stooped down and snatched it off.

'Better let it burn,' said the soldier solemnly.

'If you don't want it, Morris,' said the other, 'give it to me.'

'I won't,' said his friend doggedly. 'I threw it on the fire. If you keep it, don't blame me for what happens. Pitch it on the fire again like a sensible man.'

The other shook his head and examined his new possession closely. 'How do you do it?' he inquired.

'Hold it up in your right hand and wish aloud,' said the sergeant-major, 'but I warn you of the consequences.'

'Sounds like the *Arabian Nights*,' said Mrs White, as she rose and began to set the supper. 'Don't you think you might wish for four pairs of hands for me?'

Her husband drew the talisman from his pocket, and then all three burst into laughter as the sergeant-major, with a look of alarm on his face, caught him by the arm.

'If you must wish,' he said gruffly, 'wish for something sensible.'

Mr White dropped it back in his pocket, and placing chairs, motioned his friend to the table. In the business of supper the talisman was partly forgotten, and afterward the three sat listening in an enthralled fashion to a second instalment of the soldier's adventures in India.

'If the tale about the monkey's paw is not more truthful than those he has been telling us,' said Herbert, as the door closed behind their guest, just in time to catch the last train, 'we shan't make much out of it.'

'Did you give him anything for it, father?' inquired Mrs White, regarding her husband closely.

'A trifle,' said he, colouring slightly. 'He didn't want it, but I made him take it. And he pressed me again to throw it away.'

'Likely,' said Herbert, with pretended horror. 'Why, we're going to be rich, and famous, and happy. Wish to be an emperor, father, to begin with; then you can't be henpecked.'

He darted round the table, pursued by the maligned Mrs White armed with an antimacassar.

Mr White took the paw from his pocket and eyed it dubiously. 'I don't know what to wish for, and that's a fact,' he said slowly. 'It seems to me I've got all I want.'

'If you only cleared the house, you'd be quite happy, wouldn't you!' said Herbert, with his hand on his shoulder. 'Well, wish for two hundred pounds, then; that'll just do it.'

His father, smiling shamefacedly at his own credulity, held up the talisman, as his son, with a solemn face, somewhat marred by a wink at his mother, sat down at the piano and struck a few impressive chords.

'I wish for two hundred pounds,' said the old man distinctly.

A fine crash from the piano greeted the words, interrupted by a shuddering cry from the old man. His wife and son ran toward him.

'It moved,' he cried, with a glance of disgust at the object as it lay on the floor. 'As I wished, it twisted in my hand like a snake.'

'Well, I don't see the money,' said his son, as he picked it up and placed it on the table, 'and I bet I never shall.'

'It must have been your fancy, father,' said his wife, regarding him anxiously.

He shook his head. 'Never mind, though; there's no harm done, but it gave me a shock all the same.'

They sat down by the fire again while the two men finished their pipes. Outside, the wind was higher than ever, and the old man started nervously at the sound of a door banging upstairs. A silence unusual and depressing settled upon all three, which lasted until the old couple rose to retire for the night.

'I expect you'll find the cash tied up in a big bag in the middle of your bed,' said Herbert, as he bade them good night, 'and something horrible squatting up on top of the wardrobe watching you as you pocket your ill-gotten gains.'

He sat alone in the darkness, gazing at the dying fire, and seeing faces in it. The last face was so horrible and so simian that he gazed at it in amazement. It got so vivid that, with a little uneasy laugh, he felt on the table for a glass containing a little water to throw over it. His hand grasped the monkey's paw, and with a little shiver he wiped his hand on his coat and went up to bed.

II

In the brightness of the wintry sun next morning as it streamed over the breakfast table he laughed at his fears. There was an air of prosaic wholesomeness about the room which it had lacked on the previous night, and the dirty, shrivelled little paw was pitched on the side-board with a carelessness which betokened no great belief in its virtues.

'I suppose all old soldiers are the same,' said Mrs White. 'The idea of our listening to such nonsense! How could wishes be granted in these days? And if they could, how could two hundred pounds hurt you, father?'

'Might drop on his head from the sky,' said the frivolous Herbert.

'Morris said the things happened so naturally,' said his father, 'that you might if you so wished attribute it to coincidence.'

'Well, don't break into the money before I come back,' said Herbert as he rose from the table. 'I'm afraid it'll turn you into a mean, avaricious man, and we shall have to disown you.'

His mother laughed, and following him to the door, watched him down the road; and returning to the breakfast table, was very happy at the expense of her husband's credulity. All of which did not prevent her from scurrying to the door at the postman's knock, nor prevent her from referring somewhat shortly to retired sergeant-majors of bibulous habits when she found that the post brought a tailor's bill.

'Herbert will have some more of his funny remarks, I expect, when he comes home,' she said, as they sat at dinner.

'I dare say,' said Mr White, pouring himself out some beer; 'but for all that, the thing moved in my hand; that I'll swear to.'

'You thought it did,' said the old lady, soothingly.

'I say it did,' replied the other. 'There was no thought about it; I had just—— What's the matter?'

His wife made no reply. She was watching the mysterious movements of a man outside, who, peering in an undecided fashion at the house, appeared to be trying to make up his mind to enter. In mental connexion with the two hundred pounds, she noticed that the stranger was well dressed, and wore a silk hat of glossy newness. Three times he paused at the gate, and then walked on again. The fourth time he stood with his hand upon it, and then with sudden resolution flung it open and walked up the path. Mrs White at the same moment placed her hands behind her, and hurriedly unfastening the strings of her apron, put that useful article of apparel beneath the cushion of her chair.

She brought the stranger, who seemed ill at ease, into the room. He gazed at her furtively, and listened in a preoccupied fashion as the old lady apologized for the appearance of the room, and her husband's coat, a garment which he usually reserved for the garden. She then waited as patiently as her sex would permit, for him to broach his business, but he was at first strangely silent.

'I—was asked to call,' he said at last, and stooped and picked a piece of cotton from his trousers. 'I come from "Maw and Meggins".'

The old lady started. 'Is anything the matter?' she asked breathlessly. 'Has anything happened to Herbert? What is it? What is it?'

Her husband interposed. 'There, there, mother,' he said hastily. 'Sit down, and don't jump to conclusions. You've not brought bad news, I'm sure, sir;' and he eyed the other wistfully.

'I'm sorry——' began the visitor.

'Is he hurt?' demanded the mother wildly.

The visitor bowed in assent. 'Badly hurt,' he said quietly, 'but he is not in any pain.'

'Oh, thank God!' said the old woman, clasping her hands. 'Thank God for that! Thank——'

She broke off suddenly as the sinister meaning of the assurance dawned upon her and she saw the awful confirmation of her fears in the other's averted face. She caught her breath, and turning to her slower-witted husband, laid her trembling old hand upon his. There was a long silence.

'He was caught in the machinery,' said the visitor at length in a low voice.

'Caught in the machinery,' repeated Mr White, in a dazed fashion, 'yes.'

He sat staring blankly out at the window, and taking his wife's hand between his own, pressed it as he had been wont to do in their old courting days nearly forty years before.

'He was the only one left to us,' he said, turning gently to the visitor. 'It is hard.'

The other coughed, and rising, walked slowly to the window. 'The firm wished me to convey their sincere sympathy with you in your great loss,' he said, without looking round. 'I beg that you will understand I am only their servant and merely obeying orders.'

There was no reply; the old woman's face was white, her eyes staring, and her breath inaudible; on the husband's face was a look such as his friend the sergeant might have carried into his first action.

'I was to say that Maw and Meggins disclaim all responsibility,' continued the other. 'They admit to no liability at all, but in consideration of your son's services, they wish to present you with a certain sum as compensation.'

Mr White dropped his wife's hand, and rising to his feet, gazed with a look of horror at his visitor. His dry lips shaped the words, 'How much?'

'Two hundred pounds,' was the answer.

Unconscious of his wife's shriek, the old man smiled faintly, put out his hands like a sightless man, and dropped, a senseless heap, to the floor.

III

In the huge new cemetery, some two miles distant, the old people buried their dead, and came back to the house steeped in shadow and silence. It was all over so quickly that at first they could hardly realize it, and remained in a state of expectation as though of something else to happen—something else which was to lighten this load, too heavy for old hearts to bear.

But the days passed, and expectation gave place to resignation—the hopeless resignation of the old, sometimes miscalled apathy. Sometimes they hardly exchanged a word, for now they had nothing to talk about, and their days were long to weariness.

It was about a week after that the old man, waking suddenly in the night, stretched out his hand and found himself alone. The room was in darkness, and the sound of subdued weeping came from the window. He raised himself in bed and listened.

'Come back,' he said tenderly. 'You will be cold.'

'It is colder for my son,' said the old woman, and wept afresh.

The sound of her sobs died away on his ears. The bed was warm, and his eyes heavy with sleep. He dozed fitfully, and then slept until a sudden wild cry from his wife awoke him with a start.

'The paw!' she cried wildly. 'The monkey's paw!'

He started up in alarm. 'Where? Where is it? What's the matter?'

She came stumbling across the room toward him. 'I want it,' she said quietly. 'You've not destroyed it?'

'It's in the parlour, on the bracket,' he replied, marvelling. 'Why?'

She cried and laughed together, and bending over, kissed his cheek.

'I only just thought of it,' she said hysterically. 'Why didn't I think of it before? Why didn't *you* think of it?'

'Think of what?' he questioned.

'The other two wishes,' she replied rapidly. 'We've only had one.'

'Was not that enough?' he demanded fiercely.

'No,' she cried triumphantly; 'we'll have one more. Go down and get it quickly, and wish our boy alive again.'

The man sat up in bed and flung the bedclothes from his quaking limbs. 'Good God, you are mad!' he cried, aghast.

'Get it,' she panted; 'get it quickly, and wish—— Oh, my boy, my boy!'

Her husband struck a match and lit the candle. 'Get back to bed,' he said unsteadily. 'You don't know what you are saying.'

'We had the first wish granted,' said the old woman feverishly; 'why not the second?'

'A coincidence,' stammered the old man.

'Go and get it and wish,' cried his wife, quivering with excitement.

The old man turned and regarded her, and his voice shook. 'He has been dead ten days, and besides he—I would not tell you else, but—I could only recognize him by his clothing. If he was too terrible for you to see then, how now?'

'Bring him back,' cried the old woman, and dragged him toward the door. 'Do you think I fear the child I have nursed?'

He went down in the darkness, and felt his way to the parlour, and then to the mantelpiece. The talisman was in its place, and a horrible fear that the unspoken wish might bring his mutilated son before him ere he could escape from the room seized upon him, and he caught his breath as he found that he had lost the direction of the door. His brow cold with sweat, he felt his way round the table, and groped along the wall until he found himself in the small passage with the unwholesome thing in his hand.

Even his wife's face seemed changed as he entered the room. It was white and expectant, and to his fears seemed to have an unnatural look upon it. He was afraid of her.

'*Wish!*' she cried, in a strong voice.

'It is foolish and wicked,' he faltered.

'*Wish!*' repeated his wife.

He raised his hand. 'I wish my son alive again.'

The talisman fell to the floor, and he regarded it fearfully. Then he sank trembling into a chair as the old woman, with burning eyes, walked to the window and raised the blind.

He sat until he was chilled with the cold, glancing occasionally at the figure of the old woman peering through the window. The candle-end, which had burned below the rim of the china candlestick, was throwing pulsating shadows on the ceiling and walls, until, with a flicker larger than the rest, it expired. The old man, with an unspeakable sense of relief at the failure of the talisman, crept back to his bed, and a minute or two afterward the old woman came silently and apathetically beside him.

Neither spoke, but lay silently listening to the ticking of the clock. A stair creaked, and a squeaky mouse scurried noisily through the wall. The darkness was oppressive, and after lying for some time screwing up his courage, he took the box of matches, and striking one, went downstairs for a candle.

At the foot of the stairs the match went out, and he paused to strike another; and at the same moment a knock, so quiet and stealthy as to be scarcely audible, sounded on the front door.

The matches fell from his hand and spilled in the passage. He stood motionless, his breath suspended until the knock was repeated. Then he turned and fled swiftly back to his room, and closed the door behind him. A third knock sounded through the house.

'What's that?' cried the old woman, starting up.

'A rat,' said the old man in shaking tones—'a rat. It passed me on the stairs.'

His wife sat up in bed listening. A loud knock resounded through the house.

'It's Herbert!' she screamed. 'It's Herbert!'

She ran to the door, but her husband was before her, and catching her by the arm, held her tightly.

'What are you going to do?' he whispered hoarsely.

'It's my boy; it's Herbert!' she cried, struggling mechanically. 'I forgot it was two miles away. What are you holding me for? Let go. I must open the door.'

'For God's sake don't let it in,' cried the old man, trembling.

'You're afraid of your own son,' she cried, struggling. 'Let me go. I'm coming, Herbert; I'm coming.'

There was another knock, and another. The old woman with a sudden wrench broke free and ran from the room. Her husband followed to the landing, and called after her appealingly as she hurried downstairs. He heard the chain rattle back and the bottom bolt drawn slowly and stiffly from the socket. Then the old woman's voice, strained and panting.

'The bolt,' she cried loudly. 'Come down. I can't reach it.'

But her husband was on his hands and knees groping wildly on the floor in search of the paw. If he could only find it before the thing outside got in. A perfect fusillade of knocks reverberated through the house, and he heard the scraping of a chair as his wife put it down in the passage against the door. He heard the creaking of the bolt as it came slowly back, and at the same moment he found the monkey's paw, and frantically breathed his third and last wish.

The knocking ceased suddenly, although the echoes of it were still in the house. He heard the chair drawn back, and the door opened. A cold wind rushed up the staircase, and a long loud wail of disappointment and misery from his wife gave him courage to run down to her side, and then to the gate beyond. The street lamp flickering opposite shone on a quiet and deserted road.

The Rose Garden

M. R. JAMES

MR AND MRS ANSTRUTHER were at breakfast in the parlour of Westfield Hall, in the county of Essex. They were arranging plans for the day.

'George,' said Mrs Anstruther, 'I think you had better take the car to Maldon and see if you can get any of those knitted things I was speaking about which would do for my stall at the bazaar.'

'Oh well, if you wish it, Mary, of course I can do that, but I had half arranged to play a round with Geoffrey Williamson this morning. The bazaar isn't till Thursday of next week, is it?'

'What has that to do with it, George? I should have thought you would have guessed that if I can't get the things I want in Maldon I shall have to write to all manner of shops in town: and they are certain to send something quite unsuitable in price or quality the first time. If you have actually made an appointment with Mr Williamson, you had better keep it, but I must say I think you might have let me know.'

'Oh no, no, it wasn't really an appointment. I quite see what you mean. I'll go. And what shall you do yourself?'

'Why, when the work of the house is arranged for, I must see about laying out my new rose garden. By the way, before you start for Maldon I wish you would just take Collins to look at the place I fixed upon. You know it, of course.'

'Well, I'm not quite sure that I do, Mary. Is it at the upper end, towards the village?'

'Good gracious no, my dear George; I thought I had made that quite clear. No, it's that small clearing just off the shrubbery path that goes towards the church.'

'Oh yes, where we were saying there must have been a summer-house once: the place with the old seat and the posts. But do you think there's enough sun there?'

'My dear George, do allow me *some* common sense, and don't credit me with all your ideas about summer-houses. Yes, there will be plenty of sun when we have got rid of some of those box-bushes. I know what you are going to say, and I have as little wish as you to strip the place bare. All I want Collins to do is to clear away the old seats and the posts and things before I come out in an hour's time. And I hope you will manage to get off fairly soon. After luncheon I think I shall go on with my sketch of the church; and if you please you can go over to the links, or——'

71

'Ah, a good idea—very good! Yes, you finish that sketch, Mary, and I should be glad of a round.'

'I was going to say, you might call on the Bishop; but I suppose it is no use my making *any* suggestion. And now do be getting ready, or half the morning will be gone.'

Mr Anstruther's face, which had shown symptoms of lengthening, shortened itself again, and he hurried from the room, and was soon heard giving orders in the passage. Mrs Anstruther, a stately dame of some fifty summers, proceeded, after a second consideration of the morning's letters, to her housekeeping.

Within a few minutes Mr Anstruther had discovered Collins in the greenhouse, and they were on their way to the site of the projected rose garden. I do not know much about the conditions most suitable to these nurseries, but I am inclined to believe that Mrs Anstruther, though in the habit of describing herself as 'a great gardener,' had not been well advised in the selection of a spot for the purpose. It was a small, dank clearing, bounded on one side by a path, and on the other by thick box-bushes, laurels, and other evergreens. The ground was almost bare of grass and dark of aspect. Remains of rustic seats and an old and corrugated oak post somewhere near the middle of the clearing had given rise to Mr Anstruther's conjecture that a summer-house had once stood there.

Clearly Collins had not been put in possession of his mistress's intentions with regard to this plot of ground: and when he learnt them from Mr Anstruther he displayed no enthusiasm.

'Of course I could clear them seats away soon enough,' he said. 'They aren't no ornament to the place, Mr Anstruther, and rotten too. Look 'ere, sir'—and he broke off a large piece—'rotten right through. Yes, clear them away, to be sure we can do that.'

'And the post,' said Mr Anstruther, 'that's got to go too.'

Collins advanced, and shook the post with both hands: then he rubbed his chin.

'That's firm in the ground, that post is,' he said. 'That's been there a number of years, Mr Anstruther. I doubt I shan't get that up not quite so soon as what I can do with them seats.'

'But your mistress specially wishes it to be got out of the way in an hour's time,' said Mr Anstruther.

Collins smiled and shook his head slowly. 'You'll excuse me, sir, but you feel of it for yourself. No, sir, no one can't do what's impossible to 'em, can they, sir? I could git that post up by after tea-time, sir, but that'll want a lot of digging. What you require, you see, sir, if you'll excuse me naming of it, you want the soil loosening round this post 'ere, and me and the boy we shall take a little time doing of that. But now, these 'ere seats,' said Collins, appearing to appropriate this portion of the scheme as due to his own resourcefulness, 'why, I can get the barrer round and 'ave them cleared away in, why less than an hour's time from now, if you'll permit of it. Only——'

'Only what, Collins?'

'Well now, it ain't for me to go against orders no more than what it is for you yourself—or any one else' (this was added somewhat hurriedly), 'but if you'll pardon me, sir, this ain't the place I should have picked out for no rose garden myself. Why, look at them box and laurestinus, 'ow they reg'lar preclude the light from——'

'Ah yes, but we've got to get rid of some of them, of course.'

'Oh, indeed, get rid of them! Yes, to be sure, but—I beg your pardon, Mr Anstruther——'

'I'm sorry, Collins, but I must be getting on now. I hear the car at the door. Your mistress will explain exactly what she wishes. I'll tell her, then, that you can see your way to clearing away the seats at once, and the post this afternoon. Good morning.'

Collins was left rubbing his chin. Mrs Anstruther received the report with some discontent, but did not insist upon any change of plan.

By four o'clock that afternoon she had dismissed her husband to his golf, had dealt faithfully with Collins and with the other duties of the day, and, having sent a campstool and umbrella to the proper spot, had just settled down to her sketch of the church as seen from the shrubbery, when a maid came hurrying down the path to report that Miss Wilkins had called.

Miss Wilkins was one of the few remaining members of the family from whom the Anstruthers had bought the Westfield estate some few years back. She had been staying in the neighbourhood, and this was probably a farewell visit. 'Perhaps you could ask Miss Wilkins to join me here,' said Mrs Anstruther, and soon Miss Wilkins, a person of mature years, approached.

'Yes, I'm leaving the Ashes to-morrow, and I shall be able to tell my brother how tremendously you have improved the place. Of course he can't help regretting the old house just a little—as I do myself—but the garden is really delightful now.'

'I am so glad you can say so. But you mustn't think we've finished our improvements. Let me show you where I mean to put a rose garden. It's close by here.'

The details of the project were laid before Miss Wilkins at some length; but her thoughts were evidently elsewhere.

'Yes, delightful,' she said at last rather absently. 'But do you know, Mrs Anstruther, I'm afraid I was thinking of old times. I'm *very* glad to have seen just this spot again before you altered it. Frank and I had quite a romance about this place.'

'Yes?' said Mrs Anstruther smilingly; 'do tell me what it was. Something quaint and charming, I'm sure.'

'Not so very charming, but it has always seemed to me curious. Neither of us would ever be here alone when we were children, and I'm not sure that I should care about it now in certain moods. It is one of those things that can hardly be put into words—by me at least—and that sound rather foolish if they are not properly expressed. I can tell you after a fashion what it was that gave us—well, almost a horror of the place when we were alone. It was towards the evening of one very hot autumn day, when Frank had disappeared mysteriously about the grounds, and I was looking for him to fetch him to tea, and going down this path I suddenly saw him, not hiding in the bushes, as I rather expected, but sitting on the bench in the old summer-house—there was a wooden summer-house here, you know—up in the corner, asleep, but with such a dreadful look on his face that I really thought he must be ill or even dead. I rushed at him and shook him, and told him to wake up; and wake up he did with a scream. I assure you the poor boy seemed almost beside himself with fright. He hurried me away to the house, and was in a terrible state all that evening, hardly sleeping. Some one had to sit up with him, as far as I remember. He was better very soon, but for days I couldn't get him to say why he had been in such a condition. It came out at last that he had really been asleep and had had a very odd disjointed sort of dream. He never *saw* much of what was around him, but he *felt* the scenes most vividly. First he made out that he was standing in a large room with a number of people in it, and that some one was opposite to him who was "very powerful," and he was being asked questions which he felt to be very important, and, whenever he answered them, some one—either the person opposite to him, or some one else in the room— seemed to be, as he said, making something up against him. All the voices sounded to him very distant, but he remembered bits of things that were said: "Where were you on the 19th of October?" and "Is this your handwriting?" and so on. I can see now, of course, that he was dreaming of some trial: but we were never allowed to see the papers, and it was odd that a boy of eight should have such a vivid idea of what went on in a court. All the time he felt, he said, the most intense anxiety and oppression and hopelessness (though I don't suppose he used such words as that to me). Then, after that, there was an interval in which he remembered being dreadfully restless and miserable, and then there came another sort of picture, when he was aware that he had come out of doors on a dark raw morning with a little snow about. It was in a street, or at any rate among houses, and he felt that there were numbers and numbers of people there too, and that he was taken up some creaking wooden steps and stood on a sort of platform, but the only thing he could actually see was a small fire burning somewhere near him. Some one who had been holding his arm left hold of it and went towards this fire, and then he said the fright he was in was worse than at any other part of his dream, and if I had not wakened him up he didn't know what would have become of him. A curious dream for a child to have, wasn't it? Well, so much for that. It must have been later in the year that Frank and I were here, and I was sitting in the arbour just about sunset. I noticed the sun was going down, and told Frank to run in and see if tea was ready while I finished a chapter in the book I was reading. Frank was away longer than I expected, and the light was going so fast that I had to bend over my book to make it out. All at once I became conscious that some one was whispering to me inside the arbour. The only words I could distinguish, or thought I could, were something like "Pull, pull. I'll push, you pull."

'I started up in something of a fright. The voice—it was little more than a whisper—sounded so hoarse and angry, and yet as if it came from a long, long way off—just as it had done in Frank's dream. But, though I was startled, I had enough courage to look round and try to make out where the sound came from. And—this sounds very foolish, I know, but still it is the fact—I made sure that it was strongest when I put my ear to an old post which was part of the end of the seat. I was so certain of this that I remember making some marks on the post—as deep as I could with the scissors out of my work-basket. I don't know why. I wonder, by the way, whether that isn't the very post itself. . . . Well, yes, it might be: there *are* marks and scratches on it—but one can't be sure. Anyhow, it was just like that post you have there. My father got to know that both of us had had a fright in the arbour, and he went down there himself one evening after dinner, and the arbour was pulled down at very short notice. I recollect hearing my father talking about it to an old man who used to do odd jobs in the place, and the old man saying, "Don't you fear for that, sir: he's fast enough in there without no one don't take and let him out." But when I asked who it was, I could get no satisfactory answer. Possibly my father or mother might have told me more about it when I grew up, but, as you know, they both died when we were still quite children. I must say it has always seemed very odd to me, and I've often asked the older people in the village whether they knew of anything strange: but either they knew nothing or they wouldn't tell me. Dear, dear, how I have been boring you with my childish remembrances! but indeed that arbour did absorb our thoughts quite remarkably for a time. You can fancy, can't you, the kind of stories that we made up for ourselves. Well, dear Mrs Anstruther, I must be leaving you now. We shall meet in town this winter, I hope, shan't we?' etc., etc.

The seats and the post were cleared away and uprooted respectively by that evening. Late summer weather is proverbially treacherous, and during dinner-time Mrs Collins sent up to ask for a little brandy, because her husband had took a nasty chill and she was afraid he would not be able to do much next day.

Mrs Anstruther's morning reflections were not wholly placid. She was sure some roughs had got into the plantation during the night. 'And another thing, George: the moment that Collins is about again, you must tell him to do something about the owls. I never heard anything like them, and I'm positive one came and perched somewhere just outside our window. If it had come in I should have been out of my wits: it must have been a very large bird, from its voice. Didn't you hear it? No, of course not, you were sound asleep as usual. Still, I must say, George, you don't look as if your night had done you much good.'

'My dear, I feel as if another of the same would turn me silly. You have no idea of the dreams I had. I couldn't speak of them when I woke up, and if this room wasn't so bright and sunny I shouldn't care to think of them even now.'

'Well, really, George, that isn't very common with you, I must say. You must have—no, you only had what I had yesterday—unless you had tea at that wretched club house: did you?'

'No, no; nothing but a cup of tea and some bread and butter. I should really like to know how I came to put my dream together—as I suppose one does put one's dreams together from a lot of little things one has been seeing or reading. Look here, Mary, it was like this—if I shan't be boring you——'

'I *wish* to hear what it was, George. I will tell you when I have had enough.'

'All right. I must tell you that it wasn't like other nightmares in one way, because I didn't really *see* any one who spoke to me or touched me, and yet I was most fearfully impressed with the reality of it all. First I was sitting, no, moving about, in an old-fashioned sort of panelled room. I remember there was a fireplace and a lot of burnt papers in it, and I was in a great state of anxiety about something. There was some one else—a servant, I suppose, because I remember saying to him, "Horses, as quick as you can," and then waiting a bit: and next I heard several people coming upstairs and a noise like spurs on a boarded floor, and then the door opened and whatever it was that I was expecting happened.'

'Yes, but what was that?'

'You see, I couldn't tell: it was the sort of shock that upsets you in a dream. You either wake up or else everything goes black. That was what happened to me. Then I was in a big dark-walled room, panelled, I think, like the other, and a number of people, and I was evidently——'

'Standing your trial, I suppose, George.'

'Goodness! yes, Mary, I was; but did you dream that too? How very odd!'

'No, no; I didn't get enough sleep for that. Go on, George, and I will tell you afterwards.'

'Yes; well, I *was* being tried, for my life, I've no doubt, from the state I was in. I had no one speaking for me, and somewhere there was a most fearful fellow—on the bench; I should have said, only that he seemed to be pitching into me most unfairly, and twisting everything I said, and asking most abominable questions.'

'What about?'

'Why, dates when I was at particular places, and letters I was supposed to have written, and why I had destroyed some papers; and I recollect his laughing at answers I made in a way that quite daunted me. It doesn't sound much, but I can tell you, Mary, it was really appalling at the time. I am quite certain there was such a man once, and a most horrible villain he must have been. The things he said——'

'Thank you, I have no wish to hear them. I can go to the links any day myself. How did it end?'

'Oh, against me; *he* saw to that. I do wish, Mary, I could give you a notion of the strain that came after that, and seemed to me to last for days: waiting and waiting, and sometimes writing things I knew to be enormously important to me, and waiting for answers and none coming, and after that I came out——'

'Ah!'

'What makes you say that? Do you know what sort of thing I saw?'

'Was it a dark cold day, and snow in the streets, and a fire burning somewhere near you?'

'By George, it was! You *have* had the same nightmare! Really not? Well, it is the oddest thing! Yes; I've no doubt it was an execution for high treason. I know I was laid on straw and jolted along most wretchedly, and then had to go up some steps, and some one was holding my arm, and I remember seeing a bit of a ladder and hearing a sound of a lot of people. I really don't think I could bear now to go into a crowd of people and hear the noise they make talking. However, mercifully, I didn't get to the real business. The dream passed off with a sort of thunder inside my head. But, Mary——'

'I know what you are going to ask. I suppose this is an instance of a kind of thought-reading. Miss Wilkins called yesterday and told me of a

dream her brother had as a child when they lived here, and something
did no doubt make me think of that when I was awake last night listening
to those horrible owls and those men talking and laughing in the shrubbery (by the way, I wish you would see if they have done any damage, and
speak to the police about it); and so, I suppose, from my brain it must
have got into yours while you were asleep. Curious, no doubt, and I am
sorry it gave you such a bad night. You had better be as much in the fresh
air as you can to-day.'

'Oh, it's all right now; but I think I *will* go over to the Lodge and see if I
can get a game with any of them. And you?'

'I have enough to do for this morning; and this afternoon, if I am not
interrupted, there is my drawing.'

'To be sure—I want to see that finished very much.'

No damage was discoverable in the shrubbery. Mr Anstruther surveyed
with faint interest the site of the rose garden, where the uprooted post still
lay, and the hole it had occupied remained unfilled. Collins, upon
inquiry made, proved to be better, but quite unable to come to his work.
He expressed, by the mouth of his wife, a hope that he hadn't done
nothing wrong clearing away them things. Mrs Collins added that there
was a lot of talking people in Westfield, and the hold ones was the worst:
seemed to think everything of them having been in the parish longer
than what other people had. But as to what they said no more could then
be ascertained than that it had quite upset Collins, and was a lot of
nonsense.

Recruited by lunch and a brief period of slumber, Mrs Anstruther settled
herself comfortably upon her sketching chair in the path leading through
the shrubbery to the side-gate of the churchyard. Trees and buildings
were among her favourite subjects, and here she had good studies of both.
She worked hard, and the drawing was becoming a really pleasant thing
to look upon by the time that the wooded hills to the west had shut off the
sun. Still she would have persevered, but the light changed rapidly, and it
became obvious that the last touches must be added on the morrow. She
rose and turned towards the house, pausing for a time to take delight in
the limpid green western sky. Then she passed on between the dark box-
bushes, and, at a point just before the path debouched on the lawn, she
stopped once again and considered the quiet evening landscape, and
made a mental note that that must be the tower of one of the Roothing
churches that one caught on the sky-line. Then a bird (perhaps) rustled in
the box-bush on her left, and she turned and started at seeing what at first

she took to be a Fifth of November mask peeping out among the branches. She looked closer.

It was not a mask. It was a face—large, smooth, and pink. She remembers the minute drops of perspiration which were starting from its forehead: she remembers how the jaws were clean-shaven and the eyes shut. She remembers also, and with an accuracy which makes the thought intolerable to her, how the mouth was open and a single tooth appeared below the upper lip. As she looked the face receded into the darkness of the bush. The shelter of the house was gained and the door shut before she collapsed.

Mr and Mrs Anstruther had been for a week or more recruiting at Brighton before they received a circular from the Essex Archæological Society, and a query as to whether they possessed certain historical portraits which it was desired to include in the forthcoming work on Essex Portraits, to be published under the Society's auspices. There was an accompanying letter from the Secretary which contained the following passage: 'We are specially anxious to know whether you possess the original of the engraving of which I enclose a photograph. It represents Sir —— ——, Lord Chief Justice under Charles II., who, as you doubtless know, retired after his disgrace to Westfield, and is supposed to have died there of remorse. It may interest you to hear that a curious entry has recently been found in the registers, not of Westfield but of Priors Roothing, to the effect that the parish was so much troubled after his death that the rector of Westfield summoned the parsons of all the Roothings to come and lay him; which they did. The entry ends by saying: "The stake is in a field adjoining to the churchyard of Westfield, on the west side." Perhaps you can let us know if any tradition to this effect is current in your parish.'

The incidents which the 'enclosed photograph' recalled were productive of a severe shock to Mrs Anstruther. It was decided that she must spend the winter abroad.

Mr Anstruther, when he went down to Westfield to make the necessary arrangements, not unnaturally told his story to the rector (an old gentleman), who showed little surprise.

'Really I had managed to piece out for myself very much what must have happened, partly from old people's talk and partly from what I saw in your grounds. Of course we have suffered to some extent also. Yes, it was bad at first: like owls, as you say, and men talking sometimes. One night it was in this garden, and at other times about several of the cottages. But lately there has been very little: I think it will die out. There is nothing in our registers except the entry of the burial, and what I for a long time took to be the family motto; but last time I looked at it I noticed that it was added in a later hand and had the initials of one of our rectors quite late in the seventeenth century, A. C.—Augustine Crompton. Here it is, you see—*quieta non movere.** I suppose—— Well, it is rather hard to say exactly what I do suppose.'

---

* *Quieta non movere*: do not disturb things at rest.

Bone to His Bone

E. G. SWAIN

WILLIAM WHITEHEAD, Fellow of Emmanuel College, in the University of Cambridge, became Vicar of Stoneground in the year 1731. The annals of his incumbency were doubtless short and simple: they have not survived. In his day were no newspapers to collect gossip, no Parish Magazines to record the simple events of parochial life. One event, however, of greater moment then than now, is recorded in two places. Vicar Whitehead failed in health after 23 years of work, and journeyed to Bath in what his monument calls 'the vain hope of being restored'. The duration of his visit is unknown; it is reasonable to suppose that he made his journey in the summer, it is certain that by the month of November his physician told him to lay aside all hope of recovery.

Then it was that the thoughts of the patient turned to the comfortable straggling vicarage he had left at Stoneground, in which he had hoped to end his days. He prayed that his successor might be as happy there as he had been himself. Setting his affairs in order, as became one who had but a short time to live, he executed a will, bequeathing to the Vicars of Stoneground, for ever, the close of ground he had recently purchased because it lay next the vicarage garden. And by a codicil, he added to the bequest his library of books. Within a few days, William Whitehead was gathered to his fathers.

A mural tablet in the north aisle of the church, records, in Latin, his services and his bequests, his two marriages, and his fruitless journey to Bath. The house he loved, but never again saw, was taken down 40 years later, and re-built by Vicar James Devie. The garden, with Vicar White-head's 'close of ground' and other adjacent lands, was opened out and planted, somewhat before 1850, by Vicar Robert Towerson. The aspect of everything has changed. But in a convenient chamber on the first floor of the present vicarage the library of Vicar Whitehead stands very much as he used it and loved it, and as he bequeathed it to his successors 'for ever'.

The books there are arranged as he arranged and ticketed them. Little slips of paper, sometimes bearing interesting fragments of writing, still mark his places. His marginal comments still give life to pages from which all other interest has faded, and he would have but a dull imagination who could sit in the chamber amidst these books without ever being carried back 180 years into the past, to the time when the newest of them left the printer's hands.

Of those into whose possession the books have come, some have doubtless loved them more, and some less; some, perhaps, have left them severely alone. But neither those who loved them, nor those who loved them not, have lost them, and they passed, some century and a half after William Whitehead's death, into the hands of Mr Batchel, who loved them as a father loves his children. He lived alone, and had few domestic cares to distract his mind. He was able, therefore, to enjoy to the full what Vicar Whitehead had enjoyed so long before him. During many a long summer evening would he sit poring over long-forgotten books; and since the chamber, otherwise called the library, faced the south, he could also spend sunny winter mornings there without discomfort. Writing at a small table, or reading as he stood at a tall desk, he would browse amongst the books like an ox in a pleasant pasture.

There were other times also, at which Mr Batchel would use the books. Not being a sound sleeper (for book-loving men seldom are), he elected to use as a bedroom one of the two chambers which opened at either side into the library. The arrangement enabled him to beguile many a sleepless hour amongst the books, and in view of these nocturnal visits he kept a candle standing in a sconce above the desk, and matches always ready to his hand.

There was one disadvantage in this close proximity of his bed to the library. Owing, apparently, to some defect in the fittings of the room, which, having no mechanical tastes, Mr Batchel had never investigated, there could be heard, in the stillness of the night, exactly such sounds as might arise from a person moving about amongst the books. Visitors using the other adjacent room would often remark at breakfast, that they had heard their host in the library at one or two o'clock in the morning, when, in fact, he had not left his bed. Invariably Mr Batchel allowed them to suppose that he had been where they thought him. He disliked idle controversy, and was unwilling to afford an opening for supernatural talk. Knowing well enough the sounds by which his guests had been deceived, he wanted no other explanation of them than his own, though it was of too vague a character to count as an explanation. He conjectured that the window-sashes, or the doors, or 'something', were defective, and was too phlegmatic and too unpractical to make any investigation. The matter gave him no concern.

Persons whose sleep is uncertain are apt to have their worst nights when they would like their best. The consciousness of a special need for rest seems to bring enough mental disturbance to forbid it. So on Christmas Eve, in the year 1907, Mr Batchel, who would have liked to sleep well, in view of the labours of Christmas Day, lay hopelessly wide awake. He exhausted all the known devices for courting sleep, and, at the end, found himself wider awake than ever. A brilliant moon shone into his room, for he hated window-blinds. There was a light wind blowing, and the sounds in the library were more than usually suggestive of a person moving about. He almost determined to have the sashes 'seen to', although he could seldom be induced to have anything 'seen to'. He disliked changes, even for the better, and would submit to great inconvenience rather than have things altered with which he had become familiar.

As he revolved these matters in his mind, he heard the clocks strike the hour of midnight, and having now lost all hope of falling asleep, he rose from his bed, got into a large dressing gown which hung in readiness for such occasions, and passed into the library, with the intention of reading himself sleepy, if he could.

The moon, by this time, had passed out of the south, and the library seemed all the darker by contrast with the moonlit chamber he had left. He could see nothing but two blue-grey rectangles formed by the windows against the sky, the furniture of the room being altogether invisible. Groping along to where the table stood, Mr Batchel felt over its surface for the matches which usually lay there; he found, however, that the table was cleared of everything. He raised his right hand, therefore, in order to feel his way to a shelf where the matches were sometimes mislaid, and at that moment, whilst his hand was in mid-air, the matchbox was gently put into it!

Such an incident could hardly fail to disturb even a phlegmatic person, and Mr Batchel cried 'Who's this?' somewhat nervously. There was no answer. He struck a match, looked hastily round the room, and found it empty, as usual. There was everything, that is to say, that he was accustomed to see, but no other person than himself.

It is not quite accurate, however, to say that everything was in its usual state. Upon the tall desk lay a quarto volume that he had certainly not placed there. It was his quite invariable practice to replace his books upon the shelves after using them, and what we may call his library habits were precise and methodical. A book out of place like this, was not only an offence against good order, but a sign that his privacy had been intruded upon. With some surprise, therefore, he lit the candle standing ready in the sconce, and proceeded to examine the book, not sorry, in the disturbed condition in which he was, to have an occupation found for him.

The book proved to be one with which he was unfamiliar, and this made it certain that some other hand than his had removed it from its place. Its title was 'The Compleat Gard'ner' of M. de la Quintinye made English by John Evelyn Esquire. It was not a work in which Mr Batchel felt any great interest. It consisted of divers reflections on various parts of husbandry, doubtless entertaining enough, but too deliberate and discursive for practical purposes. He had certainly never used the book, and growing restless now in mind, said to himself that some boy having the freedom of the house, had taken it down from its place in the hope of finding pictures.

But even whilst he made this explanation he felt its weakness. To begin with, the desk was too high for a boy. The improbability that any boy would place a book there was equalled by the improbability that he would leave it there. To discover its uninviting character would be the work only of a moment, and no boy would have brought it so far from its shelf.

Mr Batchel had, however, come to read, and habit was too strong with him to be wholly set aside. Leaving 'The Compleat Gard'ner' on the desk, he turned round to the shelves to find some more congenial reading.

Hardly had he done this when he was startled by a sharp rap upon the desk behind him, followed by a rustling of paper. He turned quickly about and saw the quarto lying open. In obedience to the instinct of the moment, he at once sought a natural cause for what he saw. Only a wind, and that of the strongest, could have opened the book, and laid back its heavy cover; and though he accepted, for a brief moment, that explanation, he was too candid to retain it longer. The wind out of doors was very light. The window sash was closed and latched, and, to decide the matter finally, the book had its back, and not its edges, turned towards the only quarter from which a wind could strike.

Mr Batchel approached the desk again and stood over the book. With increasing perturbation of mind (for he still thought of the matchbox) he looked upon the open page. Without much reason beyond that he felt constrained to do something, he read the words of the half completed sentence at the turn of the page—

'at dead of night he left the house and passed into the solitude of the garden.'

But he read no more, nor did he give himself the trouble of discovering whose midnight wandering was being described, although the habit was singularly like one of his own. He was in no condition for reading, and turning his back upon the volume he slowly paced the length of the chamber, 'wondering at that which had come to pass.'

He reached the opposite end of the chamber and was in the act of turning, when again he heard the rustling of paper, and by the time he had faced round, saw the leaves of the book again turning over. In a moment the volume lay at rest, open in another place, and there was no further movement as he approached it. To make sure that he had not been deceived, he read again the words as they entered the page. The author was following a not uncommon practice of the time, and throwing common speech into forms suggested by Holy Writ: 'So dig,' it said, 'that ye may obtain.'

This passage, which to Mr Batchel seemed reprehensible in its levity, excited at once his interest and his disapproval. He was prepared to read more, but this time was not allowed. Before his eye could pass beyond the passage already cited, the leaves of the book slowly turned again, and presented but a termination of five words and a colophon.

The words were, 'to the North, an Ilex.' These three passages, in which he saw no meaning and no connection, began to entangle themselves together in Mr Batchel's mind. He found himself repeating them in different orders, now beginning with one, and now with another. Any further attempt at reading he felt to be impossible, and he was in no mind for any more experiences of the unaccountable. Sleep was, of course, further from him than ever, if that were conceivable. What he did, therefore, was to blow out the candle, to return to his moonlit bedroom, and put on more clothing, and then to pass downstairs with the object of going out of doors.

It was not unusual with Mr Batchel to walk about his garden at nighttime. This form of exercise had often, after a wakeful hour, sent him back to his bed refreshed and ready for sleep. The convenient access to the garden at such times lay through his study, whose French windows opened on to a short flight of steps, and upon these he now paused for a moment to admire the snow-like appearance of the lawns, bathed as they were in the moonlight. As he paused, he heard the city clocks strike the half-hour after midnight, and he could not forbear repeating aloud

'At dead of night he left the house, and passed into the solitude of the garden.'

It was solitary enough. At intervals the screech of an owl, and now and then the noise of a train, seemed to emphasise the solitude by drawing attention to it and then leaving it in possession of the night. Mr Batchel found himself wondering and conjecturing what Vicar Whitehead, who had acquired the close of land to secure quiet and privacy for a garden, would have thought of the railways to the west and north. He turned his face northwards, whence a whistle had just sounded, and saw a tree beautifully outlined against the sky. His breath caught at the sight. Not because the tree was unfamiliar. Mr Batchel knew all his trees. But what he had seen was 'to the North, an Ilex.'

Mr Batchel knew not what to make of it all. He had walked into the garden hundreds of times and as often seen the Ilex, but the words out of

'The Compleat Gard'ner' seemed to be pursuing him in a way that made him almost afraid. His temperament, however, as has been said already, was phlegmatic. It was commonly said, and Mr Batchel approved the verdict, whilst he condemned its inexactness, that 'his nerves were made of fiddle-string', so he braced himself afresh and set upon his walk round the silent garden, which he was accustomed to begin in a northerly direction, and was now too proud to change. He usually passed the Ilex at the beginning of his perambulation, and so would pass it now.

He did not pass it. A small discovery, as he reached it, annoyed and disturbed him. His gardener, as careful and punctilious as himself, never failed to house all his tools at the end of a day's work. Yet there, under the Ilex, standing upright in moonlight brilliant enough to cast a shadow of it, was a spade.

Mr Batchel's second thought was one of relief. After his extraordinary experiences in the library (he hardly knew now whether they had been real or not) something quite commonplace would act sedatively, and he determined to carry the spade to the tool-house.

The soil was quite dry, and the surface even a little frozen, so Mr Batchel left the path, walked up to the spade, and would have drawn it towards him. But it was as if he had made the attempt upon the trunk of the Ilex itself. The spade would not be moved. Then, first with one hand, and then with both, he tried to raise it, and still it stood firm. Mr Batchel, of course, attributed this to the frost, slight as it was. Wondering at the spade's being there, and annoyed at its being frozen, he was about to leave it and continue his walk, when the remaining words of 'The Compleat Gard'ner' seemed rather to utter themselves, than to await his will—

'So dig, that ye may obtain.'

Mr Batchel's power of independent action now deserted him. He took the spade, which no longer resisted, and began to dig. 'Five spadefuls and no more,' he said aloud. 'This is all foolishness.'

Four spadefuls of earth he then raised and spread out before him in the moonlight. There was nothing unusual to be seen. Nor did Mr Batchel decide what he would look for, whether coins, jewels, documents in canisters, or weapons. In point of fact, he dug against what he deemed his better judgement, and expected nothing. He spread before him the fifth and last spadeful of earth, not quite without result, but with no result that was at all sensational. The earth contained a bone. Mr Batchel's knowledge of anatomy was sufficient to show him that it was a human bone. He identified it, even by moonlight, as the *radius*, a bone of the forearm, as he removed the earth from it, with his thumb.

Such a discovery might be thought worthy of more than the very ordinary interest Mr Batchel showed. As a matter of fact, the presence of a human bone was easily to be accounted for. Recent excavations within the church had caused the upturning of numberless bones, which had been collected and reverently buried. But an earth-stained bone is also easily overlooked, and this *radius* had obviously found its way into the garden with some of the earth brought out of the church.

Mr Batchel was glad, rather than regretful at this termination to his adventure. He was once more provided with something to do. The re-interment of such bones as this had been his constant care, and he decided at once to restore the bone to consecrated earth. The time seemed opportune. The eyes of the curious were closed in sleep, he himself was still alert and wakeful. The spade remained by his side and the bone in his hand. So he betook himself, there and then, to the churchyard. By the still generous light of the moon, he found a place where the earth yielded to his spade, and within a few minutes the bone was laid decently to earth, some 18 inches deep.

The city clocks struck one as he finished. The whole world seemed asleep, and Mr Batchel slowly returned to the garden with his spade. As he hung it in its accustomed place he felt stealing over him the welcome desire to sleep. He walked quietly on to the house and ascended to his room. It was now dark: the moon had passed on and left the room in shadow. He lit a candle, and before undressing passed into the library. He had an irresistible curiosity to see the passages in John Evelyn's book which had so strangely adapted themselves to the events of the past hour.

In the library a last surprise awaited him. The desk upon which the book had lain was empty. 'The Compleat Gard'ner' stood in its place on the shelf. And then Mr Batchel knew that he had handled a bone of William Whitehead, and that in response to his own entreaty.

The Confession of Charles Linkworth

E. F. BENSON

DR TEESDALE HAD occasion to attend the condemned man once or twice during the week before his execution, and found him, as is often the case, when his last hope of life has vanished, quiet and perfectly resigned to his fate, and not seeming to look forward with any dread to the morning that each hour that passed brought nearer and nearer. The bitterness of death appeared to be over for him: it was done with when he was told that his appeal was refused. But for those days while hope was not yet quite abandoned, the wretched man had drunk of death daily. In all his experience the doctor had never seen a man so wildly and passionately tenacious of life, nor one so strongly knit to this material world by the sheer animal lust of living. Then the news that hope could no longer be entertained was told him, and his spirit passed out of the grip of that agony of torture and suspense, and accepted the inevitable with indifference. Yet the change was so extraordinary that it seemed to the doctor rather that the news had completely stunned his powers of feeling, and he was below the numbed surface, still knit into material things as strongly as ever. He had fainted when the result was told him, and Dr Teesdale had been called in to attend him. But the fit was but transient, and he came out of it into full consciousness of what had happened.

The murder had been a deed of peculiar horror, and there was nothing of sympathy in the mind of the public towards the perpetrator. Charles Linkworth, who now lay under capital sentence, was the keeper of a small stationery store in Sheffield, and there lived with him his wife and mother. The latter was the victim of his atrocious crime; the motive of it being to get possession of the sum of five hundred pounds, which was this woman's property. Linkworth, as came out at the trial, was in debt to the extent of a hundred pounds at the time, and during his wife's absence from home on a visit to relations, he strangled his mother, and during the night buried the body in the small back-garden of his house. On his wife's return, he had a sufficiently plausible tale to account for the elder Mrs Linkworth's disappearance, for there had been constant jarrings and bickerings between him and his mother for the last year or two, and she had more than once threatened to withdraw herself and the eight shillings a week which she contributed to household expenses, and purchase an annuity with her money. It was true, also, that during the younger Mrs Linkworth's absence from home, mother and son had had a violent quarrel arising originally from some trivial point in household management, and that in consequence of this, she had actually drawn her money out of the bank, intending to leave Sheffield next day and settle in London, where she had friends. That evening she told him this, and during the night he killed her.

His next step, before his wife's return, was logical and sound. He packed up all his mother's possessions and took them to the station, from which he saw them despatched to town by passenger train, and in the evening he asked several friends in to supper, and told them of his mother's departure. He did not (logically also, and in accordance with what they probably already knew) feign regret, but said that he and she had never got on well together, and that the cause of peace and quietness was furthered by her going. He told the same story to his wife on her return, identical in every detail, adding, however, that the quarrel had been a violent one, and that his mother had not even left him her address. This again was wisely thought of: it would prevent his wife from writing to her. She appeared to accept his story completely: indeed there was nothing strange or suspicious about it.

For a while he behaved with the composure and astuteness which most criminals possess up to a certain point, the lack of which, after that, is generally the cause of their detection. He did not, for instance, immediately pay off his debts, but took into his house a young man as lodger, who occupied his mother's room, and he dismissed the assistant in his shop, and did the entire serving himself. This gave the impression of economy, and at the same time he openly spoke of the great improvement in his trade, and not till a month had passed did he cash any of the bank-notes which he had found in a locked drawer in his mother's room. Then he changed two notes of fifty pounds and paid off his creditors.

At that point his astuteness and composure failed him. He opened a deposit account at a local bank with four more fifty-pound notes, instead of being patient, and increasing his balance at the savings bank pound by pound, and he got uneasy about that which he had buried deep enough for security in the back garden. Thinking to render himself safer in this regard, he ordered a cartload of slag and stone fragments, and with the help of his lodger employed the summer evenings when work was over in building a sort of rockery over the spot. Then came the chance circumstance which really set match to this dangerous train. There was a fire in the lost luggage office at King's Cross Station (from which he ought to have claimed his mother's property) and one of the two boxes was partially burned. The company was liable for compensation, and his mother's name on her linen, and a letter with the Sheffield address on it, led to the arrival of a purely official and formal notice, stating that the company were prepared to consider claims. It was directed to Mrs Linkworth, and Charles Linkworth's wife received and read it.

It seemed a sufficiently harmless document, but it was endorsed with his death-warrant. For he could give no explanation at all of the fact of the boxes still lying at King's Cross Station, beyond suggesting that some accident had happened to his mother. Clearly he had to put the matter in the hands of the police, with a view to tracing her movements, and if it proved that she was dead, claiming her property, which she had already drawn out of the bank. Such at least was the course urged on him by his wife and lodger, in whose presence the communication from the railway officials was read out, and it was impossible to refuse to take it. Then the silent, uncreaking machinery of justice, characteristic of England, began to move forward. Quiet men lounged about Smith Street, visited banks, observed the supposed increase in trade, and from a house near by looked into the garden where ferns were already flourishing on the rockery. Then came the arrest and the trial, which did not last very long, and on a certain Saturday night the verdict. Smart women in large hats had made the court bright with colour, and in all the crowd there was not one who felt any sympathy with the young athletic-looking man who was condemned. Many of the audience were elderly and respectable mothers, and the crime had been an outrage on motherhood, and they listened to the unfolding of the flawless evidence with strong approval. They thrilled a little when the judge put on the awful and ludicrous little black cap, and spoke the sentence appointed by God.

Linkworth went to pay the penalty for the atrocious deed, which no one who had heard the evidence could possibly doubt that he had done with the same indifference as had marked his entire demeanour since he knew his appeal had failed. The prison chaplain who had attended him had done his utmost to get him to confess, but his efforts had been quite ineffectual, and to the last he asserted, though without protestation, his innocence. On a bright September morning, when the sun shone warm on the terrible little procession that crossed the prison yard to the shed where was erected the apparatus of death, justice was done, and Dr Teesdale was satisfied that life was immediately extinct. He had been present on the scaffold, had watched the bolt drawn, and the hooded and pinioned figure drop into the pit. He had heard the chunk and creak of the rope as the sudden weight came on to it, and looking down he had seen the queer twitchings of the hanged body. They had lasted but a second or two; the execution had been perfectly satisfactory.

An hour later he made the post-mortem examination, and found that his view had been correct: the vertebrae of the spine had been broken at the neck, and death must have been absolutely instantaneous. It was hardly necessary even to make that little piece of dissection that proved this, but for the sake of form he did so. And at that moment he had a very curious and vivid mental impression that the spirit of the dead man was close beside him, as if it still dwelt in the broken habitation of its body. But there was no question at all that the body was dead: it had been dead an hour. Then followed another little circumstance that at the first seemed insignificant though curious also. One of the warders entered, and asked if the rope which had been used an hour ago, and was the hangman's perquisite, had by mistake been brought into the mortuary with the body. But there was no trace of it, and it seemed to have vanished altogether, though it was a singular thing to be lost: it was not here; it was not on the scaffold. And though the disappearance was of no particular moment it was quite inexplicable.

Dr Teesdale was a bachelor and a man of independent means, and lived in a tall-windowed and commodious house in Bedford Square, where a plain cook of surpassing excellence looked after his food, and her husband his person. There was no need for him to practise a profession at all, and he performed his work at the prison for the sake of the study of the minds of criminals. Most crime—the transgression, that is, of the rule of conduct which the human race has framed for the sake of its own preservation—he held to be either the result of some abnormality of the brain or of starvation. Crimes of theft, for instance, he would by no means refer to one head; often it is true they were the result of actual want, but more often dictated by some obscure disease of the brain. In marked cases it was labelled as kleptomania, but he was convinced there were many others which did not fall directly under dictation of physical need. More especially was this the case where the crime in question involved also some deed of violence, and he mentally placed underneath this heading, as he went home that evening, the criminal at whose last moments he had been present that morning. The crime had been abominable, the need of money not so very pressing, and the very abomination and unnaturalness of the murder inclined him to consider the murderer as lunatic rather than criminal. He had been, as far as was known, a man of quiet and kindly disposition, a good husband, a sociable neighbour. And then he had committed a crime, just one, which put him outside all pales. So monstrous a deed, whether perpetrated by a sane man or a mad one, was intolerable; there was no use for the doer of it on this planet at all. But somehow the doctor felt that he would have been more at one with the execution of justice, if the dead man had confessed. It was morally certain that he was guilty, but he wished that when there was no longer any hope for him he had endorsed the verdict himself.

He dined alone that evening, and after dinner sat in his study which adjoined the dining-room, and feeling disinclined to read, sat in his great red chair opposite the fireplace, and let his mind graze where it would. At once almost, it went back to the curious sensation he had experienced that morning, of feeling that the spirit of Linkworth was present in the mortuary, though life had been extinct for an hour. It was not the first time, especially in cases of sudden death, that he had felt a similar conviction, though perhaps it had never been quite so unmistakable as it had been today. Yet the feeling, to his mind, was quite probably formed on a natural and psychical truth. The spirit—it may be remarked that he was a believer in the doctrine of future life, and the non-extinction of the soul with the death of the body—was very likely unable or unwilling to quit at once and altogether the earthly habitation, very likely it lingered there, earthbound, for a while. In his leisure hours Dr Teesdale was a considerable student of the occult, for like most advanced and proficient physicians, he clearly recognised how narrow was the boundary of separation between soul and body, how tremendous the influence of the intangible was over material things, and it presented no difficulty to his mind that a disembodied spirit should be able to communicate directly with those who still were bounded by the finite and material.

His meditations, which were beginning to group themselves into definite sequence, were interrupted at this moment. On his desk near at hand stood his telephone, and the bell rang, not with its usual metallic insistence, but very faintly, as if the current was weak, or the mechanism impaired. However, it certainly was ringing, and he got up and took the combined ear and mouthpiece off its hook.

'Yes, yes,' he said, 'who is it?'

There was a whisper in reply almost inaudible, and quite unintelligible.

'I can't hear you,' he said.

Again the whisper sounded, but with no greater distinctness. Then it ceased altogether.

He stood there, for some half minute or so, waiting for it to be renewed, but beyond the usual chuckling and croaking, which showed, however, that he was in communication with some other instrument, there was silence. Then he replaced the receiver, rang up the Exchange, and gave his number.

'Can you tell me what number rang me up just now?' he asked.

There was a short pause, then it was given him. It was the number of the prison, where he was doctor.

'Put me on to it, please,' he said.

This was done.

'You rang me up just now,' he said down the tube. 'Yes; I am Doctor Teesdale. What is it? I could not hear what you said.'

The voice came back quite clear and intelligible.

'Some mistake, sir,' it said. 'We haven't rang you up.'

'But the Exchange tells me you did, three minutes ago.'

'Mistake at the Exchange, sir,' said the voice.

'Very odd. Well, good night. Warder Draycott, isn't it?'

'Yes, sir; good night, sir.'

Dr Teesdale went back to his big arm-chair, still less inclined to read. He let his thoughts wander on for a while, without giving them definite direction, but ever and again his mind kept coming back to that strange little incident of the telephone. Often and often he had been rung up by some mistake, often and often he had been put on to the wrong number by the Exchange, but there was something in this very subdued ringing of the telephone bell, and the unintelligible whisperings at the other end that suggested a very curious train of reflection to his mind, and soon he found himself pacing up and down his room, with his thoughts eagerly feeding on a most unusual pasture.

'But it's impossible,' he said, aloud.

He went down as usual to the prison next morning, and once again he was strangely beset with the feeling that there was some unseen presence there. He had before now had some odd psychical experiences, and knew that he was a 'sensitive'—one, that is, who is capable, under certain circumstances, of receiving supernormal impressions, and of having glimpses of the unseen world that lies about us. And this morning the presence of which he was conscious was that of the man who had been executed yesterday morning. It was local, and he felt it most strongly in the little prison yard, and as he passed the door of the condemned cell. So strong was it there that he would not have been surprised if the figure of the man had been visible to him, and as he passed through the door at the end of the passage, he turned round, actually expecting to see it. All the time, too, he was aware of a profound horror at his heart; this unseen presence strangely disturbed him. And the poor soul, he felt, wanted something done for it. Not for a moment did he doubt that this impression of his was objective, it was no imaginative phantom of his own invention that made itself so real. The spirit of Linkworth was there.

He passed into the infirmary, and for a couple of hours busied himself with his work. But all the time he was aware that the same invisible presence was near him, though its force was manifestly less here than in those places which had been more intimately associated with the man. Finally, before he left, in order to test his theory he looked into the execution shed. But next moment with a face suddenly stricken pale, he came out again, closing the door hastily. At the top of the steps stood a figure hooded and pinioned, but hazy of outline and only faintly visible. But it was visible, there was no mistake about it.

Dr Teesdale was a man of good nerve, and he recovered himself almost immediately, ashamed of his temporary panic. The terror that had blanched his face was chiefly the effect of startled nerves, not of terrified heart, and yet deeply interested as he was in psychical phenomena, he could not command himself sufficiently to go back there. Or rather he commanded himself, but his muscles refused to act on the message. If this poor earthbound spirit had any communication to make to him, he certainly much preferred that it should be made at a distance. As far as he could understand, its range was circumscribed. It haunted the prison yard, the condemned cell, the execution shed, it was more faintly felt in the infirmary. Then a further point suggested itself to his mind, and he went back to his room and sent for Warder Draycott, who had answered him on the telephone last night.

'You are quite sure,' he asked, 'that nobody rang me up last night, just before I rang you up?'

There was a certain hesitation in the man's manner which the doctor noticed.

'I don't see how it could be possible, sir,' he said. 'I had been sitting close by the telephone for half an hour before, and again before that. I must have seen him, if anyone had been to the instrument.'

'And you *saw* no one?' said the doctor with a slight emphasis.

The man became more markedly ill at ease.

'No sir, I *saw* no one,' he said, with the same emphasis.

Dr Teesdale looked away from him.

'But you had perhaps the impression that there was someone there?' he asked, carelessly, as if it was a point of no interest.

Clearly Warder Draycott had something on his mind, which he found it hard to speak of.

'Well, sir, if you put it like that,' he began. 'But you would tell me I was half asleep, or had eaten something that disagreed with me at my supper.'

The doctor dropped his careless manner.

'I should do nothing of the kind,' he said, 'any more than you would tell me that I had dropped asleep last night, when I heard my telephone bell ring. Mind you, Draycott, it did not ring as usual, I could only just hear it ringing, though it was close to me. And I could only hear a whisper when I put my ear to it. But when you spoke I heard you quite distinctly. Now I believe there was something—somebody—at this end of the telephone. You were here, and though you saw no one, you, too, felt there was someone there.

The man nodded.

'I'm not a nervous man, sir,' he said, 'and I don't deal in fancies. But there was something there. It was hovering about the instrument, and it wasn't the wind, because there wasn't a breath of wind stirring, and the night was warm. And I shut the window to make certain. But it went about the room, sir, for an hour or more. It rustled the leaves of the telephone book, and it ruffled my hair when it came close to me. And it was bitter cold, sir.'

The doctor looked him straight in the face.

'Did it remind you of what had been done yesterday morning?' he asked suddenly.

Again the man hesitated.

'Yes, sir,' he said at length. 'Convict Charles Linkworth.'

Dr Teesdale nodded reassuringly.

'That's it,' he said. 'Now, are you on duty tonight?'

'Yes, sir, I wish I wasn't.'

'I know how you feel, I have felt exactly the same myself. Now whatever this is, it seems to want to communicate with me. By the way, did you have any disturbance in the prison last night?'

'Yes, sir, there was half a dozen men who had the nightmare. Yelling and screaming they were, and quiet men, too, usually. It happens sometimes the night after an execution. I've known it before, though nothing like what it was last night.'

'I see. Now, if this—this thing you can't see wants to get at the telephone again tonight, give it every chance. It will probably come about the same time. I can't tell you why, but that usually happens. So unless you must, don't be in this room where the telephone is, just for an hour to give it plenty of time between half-past nine and half-past ten. I will be ready for it at the other end. Supposing I am rung up, I will, when it has finished, ring you up to make sure that I was not being called in— in the usual way.'

'And there is nothing to be afraid of, sir?' asked the man.

Dr Teesdale remembered his own moment of terror this morning, but he spoke quite sincerely.

'I am sure there is nothing to be afraid of,' he said, reassuringly.

Dr Teesdale had a dinner engagement that night, which he broke, and was sitting alone in his study by half-past nine. In the present state of human ignorance as to the law which governs the movements of spirits severed from the body, he could not tell the warder why it was that their visits are so often periodic, timed to punctuality according to our scheme of hours, but in scenes of tabulated instances of the appearance of *revenants*, especially if the soul was in sore need of help, as might be the case here, he found that they came at the same hour of day or night. As a rule, too, their power of making themselves seen or heard or felt grew greater for some little while after death, subsequently growing weaker as they became less earthbound, or often after that ceasing altogether, and he was prepared tonight for a less indistinct impression. The spirit apparently for the early hours of its disembodiment is weak, like a moth newly broken out from its chrysalis—and then suddenly the telephone bell rang, not so faintly as the night before, but still not with its ordinary imperative tone.

Dr Teesdale instantly got up, put the receiver to his ear. And what he heard was heart-broken sobbing, strong spasms that seemed to tear the weeper.

He waited for a little before speaking, himself cold with some nameless fear, and yet profoundly moved to help, if he was able.

'Yes, yes,' he said at length, hearing his own voice tremble. 'I am Dr Teesdale. What can I do for you? And who are you?' he added, though he felt that it was a needless question.

Slowly the sobbing died down, the whispers took its place, still broken by crying.

'I want to tell, sir—I want to tell—I must tell.'

'Yes, tell me, what is it?' said the doctor.

'No, not you—another gentleman, who used to come to see me. Will you speak to him what I say to you?—I can't make him hear me or see me.'

'Who are you?' asked Dr Teesdale suddenly.

'Charles Linkworth. I thought you knew. I am very miserable. I can't leave the prison—and it is cold. Will you send for the other gentleman?'

'Do you mean the chaplain?' asked Dr Teesdale.

'Yes, the chaplain. He read the service when I went across the yard yesterday. I shan't be so miserable when I have told.'

The doctor hesitated a moment. This was a strange story that he would have to tell Mr Dawkins, the prison chaplain, that at the other end of the telephone was the spirit of the man executed yesterday. And yet he soberly believed that it was so, that this unhappy spirit was in misery and wanted to 'tell'. There was no need to ask what he wanted to tell.

'Yes, I will ask him to come here,' he said at length.

'Thank you, sir, a thousand times. You will make him come, won't you?'

The voice was growing fainter.

'It must be tomorrow night,' it said. 'I can't speak longer now. I have to go to see—oh, my God, my God.'

The sobs broke out afresh, sounding fainter and fainter. But it was in a frenzy of terrified interest that Dr Teesdale spoke.

'To see what?' he cried. 'Tell me what you are doing, what is happening to you?'

'I can't tell you; I mayn't tell you,' said the voice very faint. 'That is part——' and it died away altogether.

Dr Teesdale waited a little, but there was no further sound of any kind, except the chuckling and croaking of the instrument. He put the receiver on to its hook again, and then became aware for the first time that his forehead was streaming with some cold dew of horror. His ears sang; his heart beat very quick and faint, and he sat down to recover himself. Once or twice he asked himself if it was possible that some terrible joke was being played on him, but he knew that could not be so; he felt perfectly sure that he had been speaking with a soul in torment of contrition for the terrible and irremediable act it had committed. It was no delusion of his senses, either; here in this comfortable room of his in Bedford Square, with London cheerfully roaring round him, he had spoken with the spirit of Charles Linkworth.

But he had no time (nor indeed inclination, for somehow his soul sat shuddering within him) to indulge in meditation. First of all he rang up the prison.

'Warder Draycott?' he asked.

There was a perceptible tremor in the man's voice as he answered. 'Yes, sir. Is it Dr Teesdale?'

'Yes. Has anything happened here with you?'

Twice it seemed that the man tried to speak and could not. At the third attempt the words came.

'Yes, sir. He has been here. I saw him go into the room where the telephone is.'

'Ah! Did you speak to him?'

'No, sir: I sweated and prayed. And there's half a dozen men as have been screaming in their sleep tonight. But it's quiet again now. I think he has gone into the execution shed.'

'Yes. Well, I think there will be no more disturbance now. By the way, please give me Mr Dawkins's home address.'

*   *   *

This was given him, and Dr Teesdale proceeded to write to the chaplain, asking him to dine with him on the following night. But suddenly he found that he could not write at his accustomed desk, with the telephone

standing close to him, and he went upstairs to the drawing-room which
he seldom used, except when he entertained his friends. There he recap-
tured the serenity of his nerves, and could control his hand. The note
simply asked Mr Dawkins to dine with him next night, when he wished
to tell him a very strange history and ask his help. 'Even if you have any
other engagement,' he concluded, 'I seriously request you to give it up.
Tonight, I did the same. I should bitterly have regretted it if I had not.'

Next night accordingly, the two sat at their dinner in the doctor's
dining-room, and when they were left to their cigarettes and coffee the
doctor spoke.

'You must not think me mad, my dear Dawkins,' he said, 'when you
hear what I have got to tell you.'

Mr Dawkins laughed.

'I will certainly promise not to do that,' he said.

'Good. Last night and the night before, a little later in the evening
than this, I spoke through the telephone with the spirit of the man we saw
executed two days ago. Charles Linkworth.'

The chaplain did not laugh. He pushed back his chair, looking
annoyed.

'Teesdale,' he said, 'is it to tell me this—I don't want to be rude—but
this bogey-tale that you have brought me here this evening?'

'Yes. You have not heard half of it. He asked me last night to get hold of
you. He wants to tell you something. We can guess, I think, what it is.'

Dawkins got up.

'Please let me hear no more of it,' he said. 'The dead do not return. In
what state or under what condition they exist has not been revealed to us.
But they have done with all material things.'

'But I must tell you more,' said the doctor. 'Two nights ago I was rung
up, but very faintly, and could only hear whispers. I instantly inquired
where the call came from and was told it came from the prison. I rang up
the prison, and Warder Draycott told me that nobody had rung me up.
He, too, was conscious of a presence.'

'I think that man drinks,' said Dawkins, sharply.

The doctor paused a moment.

'My dear fellow, you should not say that sort of thing,' he said. 'He is
one of the steadiest men we have got. And if he drinks, why not I also?'

The chaplain sat down again.

'You must forgive me,' he said, 'but I can't go into this. These are
dangerous matters to meddle with. Besides, how do you know it is not a
hoax?'

'Played by whom?' asked the doctor. 'Hark!'

The telephone bell suddenly rang. It was clearly audible to the doctor.

'Don't you hear it?' he said.

'Hear what?'

'The telephone bell ringing.'

'I hear no bell,' said the chaplain, rather angrily. 'There is no bell ringing.'

The doctor did not answer, but went through into his study, and turned on the lights. Then he took the receiver and mouthpiece off its hook.

'Yes?' he said, in a voice that trembled. 'Who is it? Yes: Mr Dawkins is here. I will try and get him to speak to you.'

He went back into the other room.

'Dawkins,' he said, 'there is a soul in agony. I pray you to listen. For God's sake come and listen.'

The chaplain hesitated a moment.

'As you will,' he said.

He took up the receiver and put it to his ear.

'I am Mr Dawkins,' he said.

He waited.

'I can hear nothing whatever,' he said at length. 'Ah, there was something there. The faintest whisper.'

'Ah, try to hear, try to hear!' said the doctor.

Again the chaplain listened. Suddenly he laid the instrument down, frowning.

'Something—somebody said, "I killed her, I confess it. I want to be forgiven." It's a hoax, my dear Teesdale. Somebody knowing your spiritualistic leanings is playing a very grim joke on you. I *can't* believe it.'

Dr Teesdale took up the receiver.

'I am Dr Teesdale,' he said. 'Can you give Mr Dawkins some sign that it is you?'

Then he laid it down again.

'He says he thinks he can,' he said. 'We must wait.'

The evening was again very warm, and the window into the paved yard at the back of the house was open. For five minutes or so the two men stood in silence, waiting, and nothing happened. Then the chaplain spoke.

'I think that is sufficiently conclusive,' he said.

Even as he spoke a very cold draught of air suddenly blew into the room, making the papers on the desk rustle. Dr Teesdale went to the window and closed it.

'Did you feel that?' he asked.

'Yes, a breath of air. Chilly.'

Once again in the closed room it stirred again.

'And did you feel that?' asked the doctor.

The chaplain nodded. He felt his heart hammering in his throat suddenly.

'Defend us from all peril and danger of this coming night,' he exclaimed.

'Something is coming!' said the doctor.

As he spoke it came. In the centre of the room not three yards away from them stood the figure of a man with his head bent over on to his shoulder, so that the face was not visible. Then he took his head in both his hands and raised it like a weight, and looked them in the face. The eyes and tongue protruded, a livid mark was round the neck. Then there came a sharp rattle on the boards of the floor, and the figure was no longer there. But on the floor there lay a new rope.

For a long while neither spoke. The sweat poured off the doctor's face, and the chaplain's white lips whispered prayers. Then by a huge effort the doctor pulled himself together. He pointed at the rope.

'It has been missing since the execution,' he said.

Then again the telephone bell rang. This time the chaplain needed no prompting. He went to it at once and the ringing ceased. For a while he listened in silence.

'Charles Linkworth,' he said at length, 'in the sight of God, in whose presence you stand, are you truly sorry for your sin?'

Some answer inaudible to the doctor came, and the chaplain closed his eyes. And Dr Teesdale knelt as he heard the words of the Absolution.

At the close there was silence again.

'I can hear nothing more,' said the chaplain, replacing the receiver.

Presently the doctor's man-servant came in with the tray of spirits and syphon. Dr Teesdale pointed without looking to where the apparition had been.

'Take the rope that is there and burn it, Parker,' he said.

There was a moment's silence.

'There is no rope, sir,' said Parker.

DOVER·THRIFT·EDITIONS

All books complete and unabridged. All 5³/₁₆″ × 8¼″, paperbound.
Just $1.00–$2.00 in U.S.A.

POETRY

DOVER BEACH AND OTHER POEMS, Matthew Arnold. 112pp. 28037-3 $1.00

BHAGAVADGITA, Bhagavadgita. 112pp. 27782-8 $1.00

SONGS OF INNOCENCE AND SONGS OF EXPERIENCE, William Blake. 64pp. 27051-3 $1.00

SONNETS FROM THE PORTUGUESE AND OTHER POEMS, Elizabeth Barrett Browning. 64pp. 27052-1 $1.00

MY LAST DUCHESS AND OTHER POEMS, Robert Browning. 128pp. 27783-6 $1.00

POEMS AND SONGS, Robert Burns. 96pp. 26863-2 $1.00

SELECTED POEMS, George Gordon, Lord Byron. 112pp. 27784-4 $1.00

THE RIME OF THE ANCIENT MARINER AND OTHER POEMS, Samuel Taylor Coleridge. 80pp. 27266-4 $1.00

SELECTED POEMS, Emily Dickinson. 64pp. 26466-1 $1.00

SELECTED POEMS, John Donne. 96pp. 27788-7 $1.00

THE RUBÁIYÁT OF OMAR KHAYYÁM: FIRST AND FIFTH EDITIONS, Edward FitzGerald. 64pp. 26467-X $1.00

A BOY'S WILL AND NORTH OF BOSTON, Robert Frost. 112pp. (Available in U.S. only.) 26866-7 $1.00

THE ROAD NOT TAKEN AND OTHER POEMS, Robert Frost. 64pp. (Available in U.S. only) 27550-7 $1.00

A SHROPSHIRE LAD, A. E. Housman. 64pp. 26468-8 $1.00

LYRIC POEMS, John Keats. 80pp. 26871-3 $1.00

THE BOOK OF PSALMS, King James Bible. 128pp. 27541-8 $1.00

GUNGA DIN AND OTHER FAVORITE POEMS, Rudyard Kipling. 80pp. 26471-8 $1.00

THE CONGO AND OTHER POEMS, Vachel Lindsay. 96pp. 27272-9 $1.00

FAVORITE POEMS, Henry Wadsworth Longfellow. 96pp. 27273-7 $1.00

SPOON RIVER ANTHOLOGY, Edgar Lee Masters. 144pp. 27275-3 $1.00

RENASCENCE AND OTHER POEMS, Edna St. Vincent Millay. 64pp. (Available in U.S. only.) 26873-X $1.00

SELECTED POEMS, John Milton. 128pp. 27554-X $1.00

GREAT SONNETS, Paul Negri (ed.). 96pp. 28052-7 $1.00

THE RAVEN AND OTHER FAVORITE POEMS, Edgar Allan Poe. 64pp. 26685-0 $1.00

ESSAY ON MAN AND OTHER POEMS, Alexander Pope. 128pp. 28053-5 $1.00

GOBLIN MARKET AND OTHER POEMS, Christina Rossetti. 64pp. 28055-1 $1.00

CHICAGO POEMS, Carl Sandburg. 80pp. 28057-8 $1.00

THE SHOOTING OF DAN MCGREW AND OTHER POEMS, Robert Service. 96pp. 27556-6 $1.00

COMPLETE SONGS FROM THE PLAYS, William Shakespeare. 80pp. 27801-8 $1.00

COMPLETE SONNETS, William Shakespeare. 80pp. 26686-9 $1.00

SELECTED POEMS, Percy Bysshe Shelley. 128pp. 27558-2 $1.00

SELECTED POEMS, Alfred Lord Tennyson. 112pp. 27282-6 $1.00

CHRISTMAS CAROLS: COMPLETE VERSES, Shane Weller (ed.). 64pp. 27397-0 $1.00

All books complete and unabridged. All 5³⁄₁₆″ × 8¼″, paperbound.
Just $1.00–$2.00 in U.S.A.

POETRY (continued)

GREAT LOVE POEMS, Shane Weller (ed.). 128pp. 27284-2 $1.00

SELECTED POEMS, Walt Whitman. 128pp. 26878-0 $1.00

THE BALLAD OF READING GAOL AND OTHER POEMS, Oscar Wilde. 64pp. 27072-6 $1.00

FAVORITE POEMS, William Wordsworth. 80pp. 27073-4 $1.00

EARLY POEMS, William Butler Yeats. 128pp. 27808-5 $1.00

FICTION

FLATLAND: A ROMANCE OF MANY DIMENSIONS, Edwin A. Abbott. 96pp. 27263-X $1.00

BEOWULF, Beowulf (trans. by R. K. Gordon). 64pp. 27264-8 $1.00

CIVIL WAR STORIES, Ambrose Bierce. 128pp. 28038-1 $1.00

ALICE'S ADVENTURES IN WONDERLAND, Lewis Carroll. 96pp. 27543-4 $1.00

O PIONEERS!, Willa Cather. 128pp. 27785-2 $1.00

FIVE GREAT SHORT STORIES, Anton Chekhov. 96pp. 26463-7 $1.00

FAVORITE FATHER BROWN STORIES, G. K. Chesterton. 96pp. 27545-0 $1.00

THE AWAKENING, Kate Chopin. 128pp. 27786-0 $1.00

HEART OF DARKNESS, Joseph Conrad. 80pp. 26464-5 $1.00

THE SECRET SHARER AND OTHER STORIES, Joseph Conrad. 128pp. 27546-9 $1.00

THE OPEN BOAT AND OTHER STORIES, Stephen Crane. 128pp. 27547-7 $1.00

THE RED BADGE OF COURAGE, Stephen Crane. 112pp. 26465-3 $1.00

A CHRISTMAS CAROL, Charles Dickens. 80pp. 26865-9 $1.00

THE CRICKET ON THE HEARTH AND OTHER CHRISTMAS STORIES, Charles Dickens. 128pp. 28039-X $1.00

NOTES FROM THE UNDERGROUND, Fyodor Dostoyevsky. 96pp. 27053-X $1.00

SIX GREAT SHERLOCK HOLMES STORIES, Sir Arthur Conan Doyle. 112pp. 27055-6 $1.00

WHERE ANGELS FEAR TO TREAD, E. M. Forster. 128pp. (Available in U.S. only) 27791-7 $1.00

THE OVERCOAT AND OTHER SHORT STORIES, Nikolai Gogol. 112pp. 27057-2 $1.00

GREAT GHOST STORIES, John Grafton (ed.). 112pp. 27270-2 $1.00

THE LUCK OF ROARING CAMP AND OTHER SHORT STORIES, Bret Harte. 96pp. 27271-0 $1.00

THE SCARLET LETTER, Nathaniel Hawthorne. 192pp. 28048-9 $2.00

YOUNG GOODMAN BROWN AND OTHER SHORT STORIES, Nathaniel Hawthorne. 128pp. 27060-2 $1.00

THE GIFT OF THE MAGI AND OTHER SHORT STORIES, O. Henry. 96pp. 27061-0 $1.00

THE NUTCRACKER AND THE GOLDEN POT, E. T. A. Hoffmann. 128pp. 27806-9 $1.00

THE BEAST IN THE JUNGLE AND OTHER STORIES, Henry James. 128pp. 27552-3 $1.00

THE TURN OF THE SCREW, Henry James. 96pp. 26684-2 $1.00

DUBLINERS, James Joyce. 160pp. 26870-5 $1.00

A PORTRAIT OF THE ARTIST AS A YOUNG MAN, James Joyce. 192pp. 28050-0 $2.00

DOVER · THRIFT · EDITIONS

All books complete and unabridged. All 5³/₁₆″ × 8¼″, paperbound.
Just $1.00–$2.00 in U.S.A.

FICTION (continued)

THE MAN WHO WOULD BE KING AND OTHER STORIES, Rudyard Kipling. 128pp. 28051-9 $1.00

SELECTED SHORT STORIES, D. H. Lawrence. 128pp. 27794-1 $1.00

GREEN TEA AND OTHER GHOST STORIES, J. Sheridan LeFanu. 96pp. 27795-X $1.00

THE CALL OF THE WILD, Jack London. 64pp. 26472-6 $1.00

FIVE GREAT SHORT STORIES, Jack London. 96pp. 27063-7 $1.00

WHITE FANG, Jack London. 160pp. 26968-X $1.00

THE NECKLACE AND OTHER SHORT STORIES, Guy de Maupassant. 128pp. 27064-5 $1.00

BARTLEBY AND BENITO CERENO, Herman Melville. 112pp. 26473-4 $1.00

THE GOLD-BUG AND OTHER TALES, Edgar Allan Poe. 128pp. 26875-6 $1.00

THE QUEEN OF SPADES AND OTHER STORIES, Alexander Pushkin. 128pp. 28054-3 $1.00

THREE LIVES, Gertrude Stein. 176pp. 28059-4 $2.00

THE STRANGE CASE OF DR. JEKYLL AND MR. HYDE, Robert Louis Stevenson. 64pp. 26688-5 $1.00

TREASURE ISLAND, Robert Louis Stevenson. 160pp. 27559-0 $1.00

THE KREUTZER SONATA AND OTHER SHORT STORIES, Leo Tolstoy. 144pp. 27805-0 $1.00

ADVENTURES OF HUCKLEBERRY FINN, Mark Twain. 224pp. 28061-6 $2.00

THE MYSTERIOUS STRANGER AND OTHER STORIES, Mark Twain. 128pp. 27069-6 $1.00

CANDIDE, Voltaire (François-Marie Arouet). 112pp. 26689-3 $1.00

THE INVISIBLE MAN, H. G. Wells. 112pp. (Available in U.S. only.) 27071-8 $1.00

ETHAN FROME, Edith Wharton. 96pp. 26690-7 $1.00

THE PICTURE OF DORIAN GRAY, Oscar Wilde. 192pp. 27807-7 $1.00

NONFICTION

THE DEVIL'S DICTIONARY, Ambrose Bierce. 144pp. 27542-6 $1.00

THE SOULS OF BLACK FOLK, W. E. B. Du Bois. 176pp. 28041-1 $2.00

SELF-RELIANCE AND OTHER ESSAYS, Ralph Waldo Emerson. 128pp. 27790-9 $1.00

GREAT SPEECHES, Abraham Lincoln. 112pp. 26872-1 $1.00

THE PRINCE, Niccolò Machiavelli. 80pp. 27274-5 $1.00

SYMPOSIUM AND PHAEDRUS, Plato. 96pp. 27798-4 $1.00

THE TRIAL AND DEATH OF SOCRATES: FOUR DIALOGUES, Plato. 128pp. 27066-1 $1.00

CIVIL DISOBEDIENCE AND OTHER ESSAYS, Henry David Thoreau. 96pp. 27563-9 $1.00

THE THEORY OF THE LEISURE CLASS, Thorstein Veblen. 256pp. 28062-4 $2.00

PLAYS

THE CHERRY ORCHARD, Anton Chekhov. 64pp. 26682-6 $1.00

THE THREE SISTERS, Anton Chekhov. 64pp. 27544-2 $1.00

THE WAY OF THE WORLD, William Congreve. 80pp. 27787-9 $1.00

MEDEA, Euripides. 64pp. 27548-5 $1.00

THE MIKADO, William Schwenck Gilbert. 64pp. 27268-0 $1.00